DEATH UNDER THE BRIDGE

A VIKING WITCH COZY MYSTERY

CATE MARTIN

Cover design by Shezaad Sudar.

Ratatoskr Press logo by Aidan Vincent.

ISBN 978-1-951439-35-4

✿ Created with Vellum

CHAPTER 1

I'll admit it, I was a little intimidated at the idea of facing my first winter on the North Shore. Not that my hometown of St. Paul, Minnesota, was much further south or anything. I had walked to school on days when the air was so cold it hurt to breathe. I knew all about the importance of warm boots and layers of clothing. I had spent more than my fair share of hours shoveling snow off of driveways and sidewalks, snow that was measured in feet, not just inches. And even warm and safe indoors, there was the dryness of the air to deal with. Every doorknob was a shock hazard, and my fine red hair would spark when I combed it and needed a ton of product to prevent it from being in an electrified cloud around my head all day.

Still, the North Shore. Lake Superior. The gales of November.

Winter here was, I was certain, going to be epic.

So when we had gotten our first killing frost that zapped the last of the greenery to a dead brown and carried away the last of the glorious autumn foliage on the trees, I had prepared myself for the change of seasons. I had broken out my thickest sweaters and set my sturdy winter boots on the mat by the kitchen door.

And my grandmother had laughed at me.

"Look," I had said, pointing out the window to the barren patch that had been her herb garden. "It's past noon, and the frost is still thick and white all over everything. It's going to snow soon!"

"It's barely October," she had said.

"Maybe the gales of November are coming early," I had said, and she had laughed again.

"Ingrid, when the gales came early and sunk the *Edmund Fitzgerald*, it was the tenth of *November*," she had said.

But a week later, as I followed her along the path beside the river that took us past the meeting hall and then further up the gorge, I had to admit she had been right. That frost had come and gone and left everything in shades of brown under the yellow glare of a sun that rose later, set sooner, and generally stayed lower in the southern sky, but still put out all the heat of late August.

"Why am I wearing a hoodie and a windbreaker again?" I asked, blowing a breath up to fluff the hair off of my sweaty forehead.

"You'll be glad for it soon enough," she said, still refusing to just tell me where we were going.

"But the weather in Villmark is the same as the weather in Runde, right?" I said. "Maybe a little windier up on the hilltop, but not by much."

"Then obviously we're not going to Villmark," she said, looking back over her shoulder at me with a twinkle in her eye. In response, I just lifted a hand to indicate the path in front of her. It only led to one place: the cave behind the waterfall. She laughed and marched on ahead, her walking stick and booted feet marking out a rhythm I was hard pressed to keep up with.

Man, did my mormor have energy.

I hoisted my messenger bag higher on my shoulder and got a tighter grip on my own walking stick as the path drew closer to the spray from the waterfall and the rocks underfoot were more slippery. My grandmother had suggested I bring along my sketchbook and pencils. She hadn't explained the why for that either, but no one ever had to ask me twice to bring my art supplies along.

In the month I had spent in Runde, I had been as artistically productive as ever. I had been worried that without the pressure of art school I would slack off, but actually the opposite was true. I had less time to spend on art given my other current decidedly nonacademic studies, but what time I had was more focused than ever.

And yet, nothing I sent out into the world was coming back to me with anything besides rejection. I knew it was early days yet, and breaking into the world of book illustration was always going to be hard, but still. My teachers had always had high praise for my work. So why wasn't I a success already?

At least Jessica had offered to let me display some of my pieces in her bookstore café. I just had to pick out which ones and get them decently framed. Local art was one of the things tourists came to the North Shore looking to buy. Surely I'd sell something soon.

I stopped just inside the space behind the waterfall and waited for my eyes to adjust to the semidarkness. The ground here was quite slippery, and although I knew it was probably not physically possible or at least not terribly likely to happen, I had a persistent, all too vivid vision of losing my footing and falling into the rush of water that was already so close I could touch it.

I didn't realize I had lost track of my grandmother until I started to head into the cave on the far side of the waterfall and she appeared out of nowhere to grab my arm and pull me back.

"Where are we going?" I asked.

"You'll see," she said with a wide grin, then led me past what I thought was the only cave behind the waterfall, the one that led up to the meadow and on to the village of Villmark. Did the path we had followed up the north slope continue on the other side of the river? I thought it was just rock and water over there before, but I had never gotten a good look at it. I was only allowed to go through the cave when I was with my grandmother, and she was always in a hurry to get through to the other side.

And as I followed my grandmother, it still did look like nothing more than rock and water with no path to speak of. We were forced to walk sideways, backs pressed against slick rock and water rushing past mere inches from our noses.

But then the narrow ledge started to widen, and the path turned away from the water, following a chasm that plunged between two rock outcroppings and down into darkness.

At least the path was wide enough here for my walking stick to be of some use. I was just starting to wonder whether I should be waving it around and tapping with it like a blind person, only I wasn't sure exactly how they used that to navigate the world, when my grandmother said something I didn't quite catch.

And then she looked back at me with a grin again, this time with a small glowing ball of flame hovering over her palm.

"Show off," I said. "When do *I* get to learn spells?"

"When you're ready," she said, which was always her answer. Only she wouldn't tell me when that would be. Not even in general terms. I had no sense of my progress at all, not how well I was doing or how far along I was. I tried to get her to lay it out for me like a school syllabus with an outline of topics and a sense of the learning parameters, but she would have nothing to do with anything like that.

It was, frankly, more frustrating than not yet being able to sell my art.

"Where are we going?" I asked, not bothering to hide my growing frustration. I knew I sounded like a surly child, but I didn't care. She was provoking it, wasn't she?

"Down to the harbor," she said. My surprise that she was actually giving me an answer only grew when those words sunk in.

"Harbor?" I asked. "What harbor? I didn't know there was a harbor."

"How else do you think the Villmark fishermen get out on the lake?" she asked me.

"First of all, I didn't know anyone in Villmark fished on the lake," I said. "I thought they got all of their fish from the river."

"It's not a very large river," my grandmother said, "And they are careful not to deplete their resources. Of course, the modern world doesn't always share the same concerns. As few are the families in Runde that keep on making a living at the fishing trade, even fewer Villmarkers manage it. But it's still a tradition they won't easily surrender." The path had been taking us in a rough spiral, always heading down, although not at too steep of an angle. Just as it leveled out my grandmother turned back to smile at me again. Whatever was up ahead, she was absolutely gleeful at the prospect of showing it to me.

"What's up there?" I asked, trying to look past her.

"Just another little tradition the Villmarkers won't easily surrender," she said. "It's a bit late in the season for this, but the weather has been so unseasonably fine, they really couldn't resist one last trip out this year."

"Ha! Unseasonably fine. I told you that frost should've brought the cold weather with it," I said.

"If you say so," my grandmother said. Then she cupped her hands together, cradling the little ball of flame between them. She whispered something to it again and then puffed up her cheeks and blew on it.

The fire grew blindingly bright. If it was giving off even half as much heat as it was light, my grandmother's hands were about to get toasted. But it wasn't just getting brighter, it was swelling in size as well. Then my grandmother threw it up into the air.

I bit back a shriek of alarm, too late to keep it from echoing through the cavernous space around us. But the light was far overhead now, shooting sparks over a wide expanse of still water that was undisturbed by the sheet of falling water that separated it from the world at large.

I followed the path of the sparks down to the dozen or so small fishing boats pulled up on the gravelly shore just a few steps away from me. Were we going to push one out onto the water and paddle out to the lake? That would explain the hoodie and windbreaker I was wearing.

But then I saw it, past the beached boats, out in the center of the harbor.

A Viking ship. An honest to goodness, real-life Viking ship. It gleamed in the light from the fireball overhead, the wood polished honey-gold with a fiery heart. Its sail was flapping softly as the waterfall pulled the air out of the cave in a continuous breeze.

And on the deck were a couple of dozen Villmarkers, all dressed like Vikings of old, shaking their shields and striking them with their spears as they whooped and hollered.

I'm sure that was more about my grandmother's presence than mine, but it was still a pretty unforgettable welcome.

CHAPTER 2

*a*s I followed my grandmother along the horseshoe-shaped gravelly beach to the far side of the cave, some of the Villmarkers climbed back down off the ship to run out to meet us. The first were the Mikkelsen sisters, Kara and Nilda, with their close friend Gullveig with them. I knew the sisters well, having spent many an evening with them in the meeting hall. They were my most dedicated teachers of the variant of Norwegian the Villmarkers spoke, and of Villmarker culture in general.

Gullveig I had met a few times, but only briefly. Still, she had made a powerful impression on my mind, as I suspect she did with most people. She was both drop-dead gorgeous and completely unaffected by it. Not unaware - she knew she turned heads - merely unwilling to feel superior just because of a lucky genetic combination.

"Ingrid!" Kara cried. Even when they reached us and could stop running, she was still dancing from foot to foot. "Isn't this amazing?"

"I had no idea this was down here," I said. "You guys were holding out on me."

"Usually it's just fishing boats down here," Nilda said. "Shipbuilding is a wintertime task, and we don't take the new ships out until the spring. But *someone* persuaded the others that the weather was so fine, they should build next year's ship early."

"Someone?" I repeated. "Why do I get the impression I'm supposed to know who?"

Nilda, Kara and Gullveig exchanged a series of significant glances, but before they could choose which of them was going to just answer the question, my grandmother ruined the moment.

"Let's get on board, shield maidens," she said, touching them each on the shoulder in passing as she headed towards the dock that led to the ship.

"Come on," Kara said, slipping an arm through mine and leading me towards the ship.

"You guys look like real-life valkyries," I said, then looked down at my own windbreaker, jeans and hiking boots. "Why did my grandmother tell me to bring a jacket when there was a whole other dress code we could've gone with?"

"We'll kit you out for the spring launch, promise," Kara said. "There's a rule among us that everyone either makes their own clothes or trades something they made for clothes someone else has made. It's how we keep the old ways alive."

"I don't know the first thing about making clothes," I said. "I made a stuffed animal in home ec once. But I didn't have to weave the cloth first."

"We'll teach you," Nilda said.

"We'll do a better job with you than we did with Gullveig here," Kara added. "She can't weave to save her life."

"So you traded something for that outfit?" I asked. "It must've been something amazing. I love that shade of blue."

"Nilda traded with me," Gullveig said.

"For these," Nilda said, raising her arms to show me her armguards.

"You're a blacksmith?" I asked Gullveig.

"Just armor pieces," she said with a shrug. "Weapons are beyond my skill."

"Look," Nilda said, pulling me to a halt so I could take a closer look at one of her armguards. I saw a pattern worked into the gold, an elaborate knot-work very delicately etched in.

"Wow," I said, turning Nilda's arm so that the armguard caught the light. "I have to get good enough at something to trade with Gullveig for sure."

"Try leather working," Gullveig said. "I need a new belt pouch. This one has a hole in the bottom that opens up again, no matter how I try to repair it."

"Leather working," I said with a nod. "Got it."

"We can worry about all that later," Kara said. "Come on. The guys are waiting for us so they can launch."

"How do we get out of here?" I asked. From where my grandmother and I had emerged onto the beach to where the dock led up to the ship had been an unbroken U. The only way out was through the waterfall.

"Your mormor does a thing," Thorbjorn said as he extended a hand to help me step over the side of the ship.

"Thorbjorn!" I said. "I haven't seen you in days!" Which, sadly, wasn't unusual. In the month I had been on the North Shore, our paths had all too rarely crossed. Of course it didn't help that I had only been to Villmark a handful of times, and he nearly never made time for kicking back in the mead hall in the evenings.

"I've been in the hills," he said, which was pretty much always his answer.

Behind me, Nilda and Kara were elbowing each other, and I belatedly realized who the *someone* must be.

"This was your idea?" I asked.

"Who told you that?" he demanded, but his cheeks flaming as red as his hair pretty much answered my question. He looked past me at the others. "You three. Are you coming on board or not?"

"What, no hand for these ladies?" Nilda asked, but before Thorbjorn could reach out to her, she vaulted easily over the side, followed by her sister and Gullveig.

"All on board?" my grandmother called from where she was sitting on a little stool at the back of the ship. "Good. Boys, push us away from the dock and I'll get started."

As the men closest to the dock did as she asked, I made my way down the center of the ship to my grandmother's side.

"This is magic?" I asked her.

"The ship? No," she said.

"I meant how we're getting out through that waterfall. That has to be magic," I said. "Can I help?"

She raised a single eyebrow but said nothing. I guessed the answer was pretty obviously no. I hadn't actually learned how to *do* anything yet. I was still working, for hours a day, on just *sensing* things.

"Ingrid, come sit with me," Thorbjorn said, patting the spot next to him on the bench.

"Okay, but I'm going to make a terrible rowing buddy," I said.

"Actually, you'd be perfect," he said. "We have to even out over all the oars."

"I think you just called me weak," I said, but took my place beside him on the bench that was closest to my grandmother. Kara, Nilda and Gullveig paired up with men that I couldn't help noticing were considerably less burly than Thorbjorn. Perhaps when they were done teaching me Norwegian and weaving and all that they could show me how they got those biceps.

Then everyone fell silent, the only sound the roar of water falling before us. I tried not to be obvious about it, but I couldn't help looking back over my shoulder to see what my grandmother was doing. She looked like she was meditating, her hands resting limply on her knees and her eyes half-closed. She wasn't whispering any spells or anything. And even when I used the skills she had taught me, I didn't sense any magic around us.

Nothing was happening.

But no one else was getting restless, so I told myself to be patient.

Then my grandmother sat up straighter on the stool with a sharp inhale of breath, and I thought I saw a flash of silver from her eyes, although perhaps that was a trick of the light.

The light. There was suddenly a lot more of it. I spun my head back around to see the waterfall in front of us parting like a curtain. Everyone around me was readying the oars, and I put my hands on the oar in front of me, for all the good I'd be. The moment that curtain had parted wide enough, with no signal passing among us, everyone started to row.

I tried to help, keeping my arms moving with the rhythm Thorbjorn set, but my mind was elsewhere. Like *everywhere* elsewhere. The morning sun was shining right ahead of us, filling the cavern with light that penetrated into dozens of deeper nooks I had totally missed seeing before. Then we were passing under the falls itself, and the sight of all of that water directly overhead, tons and tons of it barreling down toward us but then just parting to fall safely to either side, was chilling.

Literally. I felt a shiver run up the back of my spine and was finally glad for my layered hoodie and windbreaker.

Then I felt the river current catch us. At first it was a chaotic spinning, but the Villmarkers on the oars knew how to keep their ship straight until we were out of the pool under the falls and into the flow of the river.

"Won't someone see us?" I asked Thorbjorn. I realized I was whispering, but when he answered he whispered as well.

"Your grandmother's magic hides us," he said. We were still rowing, but only to steer around the occasional rock, and the oars slid through the water soundlessly.

Then the Villmarker ahead of me turned to say to Thorbjorn, "that's new." He was pointing a thumb back over his shoulder and I sat up a little straighter on the bench to see over the double row of Villmarkers on the other side of the ship. I just saw something glinting in the morning light. Most of that glinting was off of the water of a large creek, but not all of it.

"Steel," Thorbjorn said with a low chuckle. "That *is* new."

"What's new?" I asked.

"The bridge," he said, but we were moving too quickly. By the time I turned my head to look again, the smaller river was behind us. Its shores and anything spanning them were now behind a thick ridge of evergreens.

"I've not been on that side of the river much," I said. "Only to see Tuukka Jakanpoika's farm, and that's further back in the gorge than this. What's funny about a steel bridge? Because you laughed just now."

"There have been a dozen bridges across that span of river since the Norwegians settled here in the 1800s," he said. "Each one has been destroyed, broken apart by axes or burned down. But steel? That's going to be trickier. Could be fun to see what happens next."

I was tempted to ask for more details, but I doubted Thorbjorn would have them. We were in Runde now, not Villmark. I made a mental note to ask my grandmother what she knew about this bridge business after we were home for the night.

I glanced back at her again. She was still sitting ramrod straight on her stool, and I could see a glistening drop of sweat running down the side of her face. The magic she was doing was a strain, more than what she did nightly at the meeting hall so that the two villages could mix with no one from Runde noticing they were drinking with, basically, Vikings.

I really wished she would let me help her more. And I really, really wished she would share with me what I needed to do to make that happen. I needed more structure in my education. Not knowing how I was doing was going to drive me mad.

"There's the lake," Thorbjorn said with a sigh of satisfaction, but my eyes were still on the shore. Or more specifically, the cabin and fishing house that belonged to Lisa Sorensen's parents. I had solved the mystery of their daughter's murder, for all the good it had done them. They lived in Runde, completely unaware of the existence of Villmark. And I had to do my part to keep it that way. The Norse village was secret and had to remain so.

But it hurt, not being able to tell them how and why their daughter had died. Not to be able to tell them that her murderer was locked away where she could never harm another again. Not to offer them any sort of closure. It had been a month, and the police must have either already stopped working the case or were about to.

I was pretty sure that if it were possible to magic away their pain, my grandmother would've done it already. But still my heart ached. I had solved the murder, but in the end that wasn't enough.

Not for the Sorensens in their grief, and not for me.

But it wasn't just that I couldn't tell them what had happened. I felt somehow like there was a task left unchecked on my to do list. But what?

CHAPTER 3

"*I*ngrid?" Thorbjorn said, calling my mind back from the gloomy place my thoughts had gone. I gave myself a little shake and then forced a smile.

"I'm good," I said. He gave me a skeptical look, and I knew if I didn't distract him he was going to start asking questions. And those answers were going to completely ruin the day he had put so much effort into. I had to find something more cheerful to say, and quick.

I looked down at the oar in my hands, its wood shining even more brightly golden in the morning sun. "Is this oar hand-carved? The end of it is like an animal claw or something."

"Everything is hand-carved," he said. "I helped with the mast mainly myself. It takes a particular kind of tree, and my brothers and I had to scour the forest to find the perfect candidate."

"Your brothers," I said, sitting up straighter to look around. Which wasn't easy; even the Villmarker women towered over me. "Are they here? I still haven't met even one of them. I'm starting to wonder if you made them up."

"Ingrid, we all six played together as children," he said, "back before we had responsibilities."

Six, which meant the five brothers plus me. Only I didn't

remember more than a few random images. I had spent an entire summer with my grandmother when I was young, exploring Villmark and its environs, only to forget it all when I went back to my mother in St. Paul. I don't know when exactly I started forgetting, if it happened all at once or slowly over time.

Strong images had stayed with me, recurring in dreams that I later turned into my illustrations. Since coming to Runde I had gone through all of my old art and sketchbooks and saw specific things I knew to be real now.

Things like the ship I was on.

"I was on a ship like this before, right?" I said.

"Yes!" Thorbjorn said. "You're starting to remember?"

"Not really," I said with an apologetic smile. "I just saw some drawings I did that I guess I didn't draw from my imagination like I thought I had."

"My brothers were with us that day, but not today," he said. "Protecting the village is a vital duty, and we take it seriously. Even I haven't seen all of my brothers together at once since the night Halldis attacked you."

"When you fought the giants," I said with a sigh. "I would rather have been there watching that."

"It wasn't much of a fight, really," he said, but I could see his cheeks pinkening in a way that had nothing to do with the intense sun reflecting off of all that water.

"At any rate, we all pitched in to craft this ship. Tasks were assigned by skill and ability. Hence the heavy lifting for me and my brothers. But anything that shows real art, that's all Solvi." Then he pointed with his chin to a Villmarker a few rows ahead of us. This man was tall, with broad shoulders and long blond hair. So basically he looked like most of the other guys on the ship.

But he heard someone saying his name and turned to see who it was. He gave Thorbjorn a little wave, his face unsmiling, then turned back to his oar.

"This is amazing work," I said, running my fingers over the grooves in the wood. I had done a little sculpting in art school, but only with clay.

"You should walk around, take a look at everything now in the sunlight," he said.

"I will. In fact, I'm guessing that's why mormor insisted I bring my sketchbook with me," I said, digging into the bag I had tucked under the bench behind my feet.

It was truly a magnificent day. The wind blowing over the water was brisk, but the sun shone down warmly in a nearly cloudless sky. As I moved from place to place around the ship, sketching not just the details of the ship but also the people around me, the Villmarkers began to sing what I guessed were rowing songs. I could catch about half of the words, and had a pretty good hunch that the half I wasn't understanding were likely quite bawdy. The raucous laughter would certainly say so.

Although we were out in the daytime, that night was going to be the full moon, and the waters were clearly feeling it. The waves grew ever higher, rolling the ship and launching it into the air before catching it again in a cold spray. I think I would've been seasick - or, I guess, lake-sick - if not for the focus I was putting on sketching what was right in front of me.

I could only imagine what it was like for our ancestors out on the ocean waves in such a ship. Massive swells, no land in sight. Their bravery was awe-inspiring.

My grandmother kept up her meditative spell the entire day. It wasn't hard to guess why; there was always a freighter on the horizon or a fishing boat or sailboat passing closer by. A ship full of costumed Vikings out on the lake would be a little hard to explain.

Lunch was a portable smorgasbord, with open-faced cold meat sandwiches and a variety of creamy salads we all passed around. Then the Villmarkers leaned in to their oars and turned the ship around to head back the way we had come. The sail snapped full, and the wind was carrying us now, and to my surprise the Villmarkers abandoned their oars and stripped off their armor to dive into the lake.

Into the freezing waters of Lake Superior. In the middle of

summer, that water was still dangerously cold. In October? Only crazy people would jump into that.

"Are you coming, Ingrid?" Kara asked as she, Nilda and Gullveig prepared to dive over the side.

"Are you kidding? Only crazy people would jump into that," I said.

"Next year she'll be diving in for sure," Thorbjorn said to them. They laughed, then jumped into the water, joining the others in splashing and diving under the waves.

I didn't have to ask why Thorbjorn wasn't joining them. It was pretty obvious he was still on duty, eyes alternating between scanning the horizon for signs of danger and counting the heads that were bouncing in the water, making sure we didn't lose anyone.

The swimming didn't last long. Aside from the water being excessively cold, the wind was carrying the ship at a fast clip, and keeping up had to be exhausting. One by one the Villmarkers came back aboard to sprawl out on the benches and let the sun dry them while they stayed low and out of the wind.

Gullveig was the last to pull herself on board, and she looked as fresh as when she had first plunged into the water, not a bit like she'd just been swimming at a sprinting pace for the better part of the afternoon.

The sun was setting behind the hills as we finally dropped the sail and took up the oars once more to row against the current, up the river to the waterfall. We reached the pool and used the oars to hold us steady and face-on with the waterfall.

Which was still falling in an unbroken sheet.

I looked back at my grandmother and to my dismay saw she was slumping on her stool. She had been using magic all day to keep us out of sight. I even thought once or twice that I could feel her exerting her will on the weather, keeping the day fine and the waves high. I hadn't spoken to her all day, since she had stayed in that meditative state which I was reluctant to disturb. But maybe I should have, at least once, pulled her out of it enough to check on her.

Was she too tired to get us all the way home again? What if she couldn't part the waterfall? Would we have to beach the ship here, in Runde? Where could we hide it?

I could hear murmurs of voices around me. I wasn't the only one who was worried, although everyone was still keeping their voices low, not disturbing my grandmother.

I looked back again. She was whispering to herself, but her hands dangled uselessly at her sides.

I had to do something.

But so far I had only been taught to sense the presence of magic, not to access it myself. What could I do?

But I *had* accessed magic before. I had seen patterns like runes that had given me clues to solve Lisa's murder. Not that seeing patterns was going to help me now.

A sudden inspiration struck me and I dug my sketchbook back out of my bag. When I had seen those patterns, I had been imagining drawing what I was looking at. But I could do more than imagine it now. I turned to a blank page and began sketching furiously. I was drawing what I saw before me, every rock and twisted tree, the pool and even the prow of the ship. I strove to get down every detail as accurately as I could.

Save one. The waterfall I drew was parted like a curtain, the water cascading down around a gap just wide enough for my sketched ship to pass through.

I ran out of details to add and just turned my attention to the shading of the water itself, rubbing the graphite from my pencil with my thumb. I was trying to keep my movements smooth like the water, but then my thumb made a little hitch all on its own.

Had I just traced a rune in the sketched water?

I started to lean in to get a closer look at the drawing in the fading light, but was distracted by a sudden cheer rising all around me. The Villmarkers shouted and clapped but quickly turned their attention back to rowing, to get the ship into the harbor before the waterfall returned to its natural form.

"Nice work," Thorbjorn said to me as I put my sketchbook away.

"I'm not sure I did anything," I said. "I don't actually know how to use any magic yet."

"Your instincts are good," he said.

The ship jostled against the dock, and a few of the men leaped over the side to tether us in place. Darkness fell abruptly as the waterfall closed behind us.

I turned to see my grandmother sitting up straighter on her stool but rubbing her face tiredly. "Mormor?" I asked.

"I'm all right," she said. "I just need a moment."

I wanted to argue. She looked like she'd just run a marathon without training for it first, really inadvisable at her age.

But I could feel something happening around me. I couldn't quite get it into focus, but I sensed that the very stone around us was passing something into my grandmother. Magic? Power? Or just a mundane sort of energy so she could get walking again?

I tried to feel where it was coming from more specifically, suspecting it was from the fire in the cave above, the one the Vill-markers never let die out, but that level of perception was still beyond me. I could sense its presence and motion, but nothing more specific.

Still, if I kept setting myself little tasks like that, I could start measuring my own progress. If my grandmother wouldn't offer me a way of measuring it, I could find my own.

"A fine day," someone said, and others agreed, getting up from the benches and slapping each other on their now-sunburned backs. But no one was in a hurry to disembark. It was like they were all holding their breath, waiting for something to happen.

"Yes, a fine day," my grandmother said, and finally dropped her hands from her face to smile radiantly at everyone. "Now, who's up for an equally fine night?"

The crowd roared its approval, and two of the larger men moved to the back of the ship to lift my grandmother up on their shoulders. They looked like football players carrying their triumphant coach off the field after the big game, but I suspected they knew as well as I that my grandmother was hiding just how tired she was from all of us.

"Can she handle this?" I whispered to Thorbjorn as the two Villmarkers carrying my grandmother led the way up to the higher cave, the rest of the group following behind in laughing and chatting clumps, the mead hall their final destination.

"She can," Thorbjorn assured me. "She would never put us at risk by pushing herself too hard. You can put your trust in that."

I nodded, but inside my own head, I wasn't so sure.

CHAPTER 4

$\mathcal{T}$horbjorn and I were the last of the group to emerge from the riverside path and walk past the sandy pits to the meeting hall's back patio.

It still looked like it always did by daylight: rain-damaged plastic patio furniture stacked against old aluminum siding, the patio itself badly cracked concrete. The weeds that fought their way up through the cracks were the same dead brown as everything else since that frost. Everything looked perfectly normal from a Runde perspective.

But it was well after sunset now. It should look different.

"It's all right," Thorbjorn said, but I think he was trying to reassure himself as much as me.

We went in through the door to find the other Villmarkers, still dressed as Vikings, gathering around badly balanced and scuffed tables. Unbothered by the drab appearances, they were pulling out plastic chairs to drag them closer to what might have been a space heater but was in no way the magnificent fireplace it should be.

And then, in a blink of an eye, it was. The rafters overhead were carved wood darkened by decades of smoke, the long tables were beer-stained wood, and the chairs were heavy benches. The fire on the hearth was burning hot and bright, and everyone gave up yet another cheer.

"It's a good thing it's too early for locals to be in here yet," I said to Thorbjorn, but he laughed and pointed to the far end of the room where a trio of farmers were looking at each other with nervous eyes. I could tell they wanted to ask each other if they had all just seen what had happened, but no one wanted to speak first.

Then one of the Villmarkers approached them with two mugs of beer in each of his hands, and they greeted him with a very relieved shout. By the time they had quaffed those beers, it was like the moment when the world around them had suddenly changed was just gone from their minds.

"Your grandmother still has it," Thorbjorn said to me.

I couldn't argue with that.

I looked around to see if any of my Runde friends were among the locals, but they weren't. Well, it was early yet, and technically a weeknight.

"Are you staying or do you have to work?" I asked.

"Staying," he said with a warm smile.

"Cool," I said, pleased. "Sit by the fire?"

"No, let's take that corner of there," Thorbjorn said, pointing out a cozy little nook in the farthest corner from the fire.

"Okay," I said slowly. I wasn't sure what this sudden change in sociability meant. I knew that he spent most of his time alone, as apparently his brothers did. But when he was with the others, he tended to be the center of everything, telling the best stories and the funniest jokes and challenging anyone at all to any sort of competition, no matter how dangerous or how mundane. Being in the mead hall, but apart from the others? How long could that even last before someone dragged him off to settle some bet?

I didn't see how it happened, but when we reached the table and I had set my bag into the corner behind my chair, I straightened to see Thorbjorn already had drinks in his hand. He had an enormous mug of beer for himself and set a comparatively dainty mug of mead in front of me.

Comparatively. As I took a sip of the honey wine, I reminded myself I was in no way going to finish this drink. There must have been a whole bottle's worth in there.

"A fine day," Thorbjorn said as he wiped beer foam from his beard, then looked around the room at his fellow Villmarkers with a radiant fondness.

"Yes, that was fantastic," I said. "I have so many sketches. Just rough drawings, but when I start fleshing them out, I'll have some amazing illustrations."

"I imagine so," he said. "The ship we were on as kids was nowhere near as beautiful as the one we made this year. That should be even more inspiring for you than the last one."

"I hope so," I said, taking another sip of my mead. "Of course things don't have the same impact on adults as they do in children. I'm an artist, so I try to keep that child alive inside of me, but it's not the same as when I was actually a child."

"No," he agreed. "That voyage when we were children, that helped your art?"

"I think it spawned it," I said. "I'm not exaggerating. Really, someday when you have a little time, you really should come down to my grandmother's house so I can show you the most impressive drawings I've done. They're really too big to be lugging around, and I could just see myself tripping and throwing my life's work into the waterfall."

"I suppose I should," he said, looking down into his own beer as if he had found something floating in it.

I could feel his disappointment, but it took me a moment to work out the cause. There was no reason he couldn't come down to Runde. He had before, if just to the crossroads. So why was he sad now?

Then it dawned on me. He had really hoped I would remember more, that the day out on the water in the ship would bring back all the memories. I wished it had, but I wasn't sad that it didn't. At least, not the way Thorbjorn seemed to be.

Was there something specific he wanted me to remember from when I was eight?

"Hey," I said, nudging his arm to break his moody regarding of his beer. "This was an unforgettable day. Seriously. I'm going to treasure the memory of it for the rest of my life. Never in a million years did I think I would ever feel what it was like to be in an actual Viking ship rolling over the waves. Thank you."

"Well, don't thank me," he said. "Your grandmother did the magic."

"I'm guessing because you asked her to," I said. He said nothing, just hastily took another long pull from the mug.

I took another sip of mead and looked past Thorbjorn to the table with the three locals. They were still with the Villmarker who had brought over the round of beers, all talking and laughing together. But there was a fifth person at their table now who was sitting with them but not really taking part in the conversation.

Roarr.

I had seen him around Villmark a few times in the last month when I had been there with my grandmother. We had never spoken to him directly, but even among the others he always seemed to keep to himself. Not that the other Villmarkers were shunning him or anything, they just didn't seem to know what to do with him.

"Have you talked to Roarr at all?" I asked Thorbjorn.

He turned to follow my gaze over his shoulder, then turned back to me with a shrug. "Not really."

"He seems lonely," I said.

"Shouldn't he be?" Thorbjorn asked.

"Maybe?" I said. "But also, he's still grieving. It seems cruel to have to go through that alone."

"He has his parents," Thorbjorn said, then set his beer down with a thunk. "You feel sorry for him?"

"I can't help it," I said, throwing up my hands. "It would help if there was some way to figure out just how much he was under Halldis' spell and how much was him just going along with things. Or taking an active part, even. I hate not knowing."

"I think the only person who can ever know all of that for sure is Roarr," he said. "He has to confront that in himself. Or not; it's all up to him." He took another drink of beer.

I looked down at the mead in the mug in front of me. I had only had a few little sips, and yet my head was already starting to feel swimmy. I was tempted to lay my head down on my folded arms and go to sleep right there on the table.

"You're tired," Thorbjorn said. I jumped, belatedly realizing I had just zoned out sitting there on the bench for I had no idea how long.

"I'm okay," I said, sitting up straighter and looking around the hall. "I was hoping some of the others might stop in later. It's too early to go home."

"After what you did today? An early bedtime is probably exactly what you need," he said. And then he took the mug of mead away from me.

"What I did today?" I said. "You mean sitting there letting you row? Watching everyone swim like crazy to keep up with a ship riding a brisk wind? Because I promise you drawing all day is how I normally spend my time, and it doesn't have me in bed by..." I glanced at my watch and winced, "eight."

"You did more than that," he said. "More than you were meant to, but we could all see that your grandmother needed you."

"I didn't do anything," I said. "I mean, I drew what it should've looked like if my grandmother's spell had been working, but that's nothing. It didn't feel like magic when I did it. It certainly wasn't exhausting."

"You're paying the price now," he said. "It's not like running from a bear. You don't get winded right away."

"You speak from experience?" I asked.

"I haven't run from a bear since I was ten," he snorted.

"I meant the magic thing," I said.

"Well, no," he admitted. "But I've spent more time than most in your grandmother's company. You might as well go home. It's going to be an early night for the rest of us, anyway. Your grandmother can't keep it up all night after the day we had."

"I should stay until she goes," I said, but I ruined the illusion of being firmly resolved in my vow by yawning hugely.

"Go," he said. "I'll watch over your grandmother for you."

27

"Thank you, Thorbjorn," I said as I grabbed my bag and got off the bench. Then, on impulse, I leaned over to plant a quick kiss on his cheek. "For the whole day. For everything," I said.

He made some sort of harrumphing noise, but a few of the neighboring tables had witnessed our little moment, and laughing and ribbing started before I had even straightened back up again.

By the time I reached the open doorway that led out to the parking lot and Runde proper, Thorbjorn had moved to one of the louder tables to sit between an ecstatic-looking Kara and a calmer Nilda. There were lining up challengers in front of him for arm wrestling.

In two lines, one for each arm.

As I stepped outside, I threw one last glance back over my shoulder toward the bar, hoping to catch a glimpse of my grandmother. If she was there, I couldn't see her over the taller heads of the men waiting for beer.

Then I collided with something large and immoveable. Strong hands caught my arms to keep me from stumbling back.

Damn that mead. Or the magic. Or both.

"Sorry," I said, trying to look my crash victim in the eye, but I couldn't quite do it. It was too dark in the doorway, so far from the fire, and he was too tall.

"Not a worry," a deep voice reassured me, and then he moved past me into the hall and I was alone on the concrete stoop.

I blinked a few times. As tired as I was, I also seemed to be more attuned to magic. Never before had I felt such a sharp distinction between being inside the hall with all the illusion magic coursing through it and being out in the mundane world.

Perhaps mead was the key. I laughed to myself as I started across the parking lot. I could just imagine the look on my grandmother's face if the next time we started a magic lesson I told her I needed a mug of mead the size of my head first.

I only stumbled a few times on the way home and let myself in through the kitchen door to immediately be greeted by a very cranky cat.

"What?" I demanded as I struggled out of my boots. "I left you with your full day's worth of food and plenty of water. Don't tell me you were lonely because, and I hate to point this out to you, you are a cat."

Mjolner made one last complaining meow. I let him have the last word since I was pretty sure I had made my point. He followed me upstairs and watched as I made an attempt at brushing my teeth and then changed from clothes that still smelled of Lake Superior into my PJs.

I climbed under the duvet and the moment I was settled, Mjolner hopped onto the bed to curl up on the part of the pillow I wasn't using. By morning his share would somehow be twice the size of mine, but for now there was nothing better for sleeping than the satisfied sound of his purr close to my ear. I could feel that purr vibrating against my neck as I drifted off.

I don't know if it was seeing Roarr, or doing that spell, or maybe just being in that cave and feeling the magic pouring into my grandmother, but the minute I closed my eyes I dreamed of Halldis.

I hadn't seen her since the night she had tried to kill me, but I knew she was somewhere in those caves. Deeper and further in than I would ever have cause to go, Thorbjorn had told me. He had meant to reassure me, but I think I would rest more easily if I could see her there and know exactly where she was.

This wasn't my first Halldis nightmare, but it was the most intense by far. Usually I just sensed her somewhere deep under the earth, and in those nightmares she was always watching me. Always aware of me, and in my dream I knew that was true when I was awake as much as when I was asleep. Those dreams were more just feelings than actual visual impressions, but somehow I sensed she was changing her appearance again, away from the crone she was and back towards the ever-youthful visage she preferred.

But this night I saw more. I saw her in a cave made up like a humble little room with a bed and a table and chair set close to a smoky fire. She was sitting in that chair, but this time she wasn't watching me. She didn't even seem to be aware of me. Her eyes were closed, and her hands on her lap were twitching. But that twitching wasn't random. It was deliberate. It looked like...

What did it look like? It reminded me of something.

A loud pounding echoed around me and my eyes flew open to find myself sitting up in my little bed in my grandmother's cabin. My heart was racing and my breath was coming fast. My throat had a raw feeling, like I'd just screamed as loud and hard as I could.

Had I?

I concentrated on slowing my breathing, and my heart rate followed. Then I looked out of the window over my bed. The sky was gray, not quite dawn. But I didn't think I was going to get any more sleep that night.

I reached for my robe, but my attention was caught by the motion of my own hand. I pulled it back then started moving my fingers, trying to trigger whatever thought hadn't quite formed the first time.

A puppeteer. A master puppeteer, one of the ones who could manipulate a marionette in each hand. The elaborate ones with lots of strings.

That's what Halldis' hands had reminded me of.

I had to draw this right away before the image faded from my mind. I turned towards the drawing easel tucked in the corner of the room.

Then the pounding came again, and I realized that hadn't been part of the dream at all.

It wasn't even dawn yet, but someone was already at the door.

I grabbed my robe and ran down the stairs, only a little annoyed that Mjolner still slept contentedly, now taking up the whole pillow.

CHAPTER 5

*R*emembering that my grandmother was likely still exhausted from the day before, I ran down the stairs to get to the door before whoever it was woke her, but I was too late. She was already there, hand on the knob to open the door. At first I thought she was still wearing her clothes from yesterday. But no, she had been wearing a blue flannel shirt yesterday, not the red and green checked one I saw now.

How many knocks had there been that I had slept through? Or had she sensed trouble coming and dressed before it even arrived on our doorstep?

I thought about going back up the stairs and getting dressed myself, but my curiosity was too strong. I lingered on the bottom step and leaned over the rail to see who was out there as my grandmother swung the door open.

"Good morning, Carl, Tobias," my grandmother said, giving a nod each to the two young men standing there. I didn't recognize them. They were both of average height and average build, dressed in the work jeans and warm flannel that was the Runde standard attire. They both had eyes the same shade of grayish-blue and light brown hair that curled at the ends but was flattened on top, presumably by the hats they currently held in their hands.

"Ms. Torfa," the one she had called Carl said. He twisted the knit cap in his hands and shot Tobias a nervous look. Tobias gave him a supportive nod. "There's been trouble down at the bridge," he said, all in a rush. "We need you to come before it gets bad."

"Trouble at the bridge," my grandmother repeated with a very weary sigh.

"The new bridge?" I said. "The steel one?"

"Yes, that's right," Carl said.

"This is news to me," my grandmother said, turning to raise her eyebrows at me.

"I saw it yesterday from the-" I literally bit my tongue before the rest of that sentence could spill out of me. "I saw it yesterday. I was going to ask you about it today, actually."

"It seems, as early as it is, we're too late for that conversation," she said, then turned back to the men on her porch. "Steel, this time? Did someone set it on fire anyway?"

"No, ma'am," Carl said.

"Everyone was at the Old Sorensen Farm all night, arguing about what to do about it," Tobias said.

"Everyone? All the Sorensens?" my grandmother asked.

"Only a few of us fishing Sorensens," Tobias said. "But pretty near all the farming Sorensens were there."

"Pretty near," my grandmother repeated as if making a mental note of that fact.

"The point is, none of us were down by the bridge when it happened," Carl said, then amended, "I mean, when it must have happened."

"When what must have happened?"

But words failed him. It was Tobias who said, "there's been a murder. We think. There's a body, anyway."

"Who?" my grandmother asked.

"We didn't stay to find out," Carl said. "We came right here."

"The body is in the creek, but sort of fetched up under the bridge.

Facedown, but it's definitely a man, and his hair looked dark to me," Tobias said.

"Dark hair, but you didn't recognize him?" my grandmother asked.

"Not a Sorensen," Carl said. "We think maybe a Nelsen."

"Who found the body?" my grandmother asked.

"Davey Sorensen," Carl said. "He's-"

"Stuart's boy," my grandmother said for him. "Sixteen now?"

"That's right, ma'am," Carl said. "He had been heading to school early, had some sort of club thing he had to get to before first bell, but went out to tend to his chores first. But then he came running back and woke the rest of us. The others are all down there now."

"The others meaning the other Sorensens?" my grandmother guessed. "No Nelsens?"

"Not when we left," Carl said. "But they're probably there by now."

"You should come quickly," Tobias said.

My grandmother gave a curt nod. "Right. Carl, you're coming with me now. Tobias, wait here for my granddaughter to get dressed and then show her the way. Ingrid, don't dawdle."

"I won't," I said, already halfway back up the stairs. I dressed as quickly as I could, pulling on the same hoodie and windbreaker as the day before, and then ran back downstairs to pull on my hiking boots as Tobias waited awkwardly just inside the door.

"I'm Ingrid, by the way," I said as I yanked my laces tight. "I don't think we've met?"

"Briefly, but I'm not surprised that you don't remember me," he said.

"Lisa's funeral," I guessed, and he nodded. I had met a lot of Sorensens that day. They all did kind of look alike, too. "You're a fishing Sorensen, right? But Carl is a farmer? I could've sworn you were brothers."

"Cousins, actually," he said. "My dad joined my mom's dad's fishing business when they married."

"How do you like it?" I asked as I smoothed down my uncombed hair and then tugged a wool hat down over it.

"It's okay," he said with a shrug. "But my dad loves being out on the lake. I can't see him farming ever, but I guess he did when he was a kid."

I gave a nod towards the door and he put on his own hat before heading back out into the chilly North Shore morning. I pulled the door shut behind me but didn't lock it, something that still felt really strange to me. It was like constantly leaving the house with the oven on and an iron plugged in and the bath running. My mind kept shrieking at me that I had forgotten something. I supposed at some point I'd get used to it.

I'd have to. The one time I had asked, my grandmother had confessed she didn't even know where the door key had gotten to, and hadn't seemed at all concerned.

The air was chilly, but the dew on the ground was still too wet to be frost. The sun wasn't quite over the horizon yet, but the sky over the lake was cloudless, just a watercolor background of blues and pinks. In any other circumstances, it would be a lovely morning for a walk.

But the circumstances were dire, and our walk was almost a jog.

The only bridge across the river that the Villmarkers called Konallelva and the people of Runde called simply the Konal was the one that carried the highway over the entire valley where Runde lay. We had to climb up the steep embankment to the crossroads where the restaurant, gas station, and bookshop café were all clustered, then cross the bridge to get to the southern side before descending another footpath to the south side of the Konal.

I had never wondered before why there was no bridge in the valley. The only thing on the south side were a few widely scattered farms. But now it seemed odd that those people didn't want a closer connection to Runde proper. Was it because the Villmarkers needed the river bridge-free to launch their Viking ship? I would have to ask my grandmother about that. Their fishing boats could fit under any standard bridge, but that ship with its tall mast would require a lot more space.

"So you're a fishing Sorensen?" I asked, and Tobias nodded. "But you still understand all the fuss about this bridge? Because I've never had it explained to me."

Tobias sighed. "You know, I think the fuss about the bridge is part of what drove my dad away from the farm," he said. "It goes back generations, like something from a novel. The Hatfields and the McCoys, you know?"

"I think those were actually real," I said.

"Maybe," he said. "All I know is, the Runde founders declared the banks of the river as common use land. Everyone needed to fish it, especially in the town's early days. But the argument is over whether that meant the banks of the creek too, particularly the large one that splits the Nelsen lands in half."

"What do the Sorensens care if the Nelsens bridge their lands?" I asked.

"Because technically they're doing it just a few feet on the wrong side of the property line," he said.

"On Sorensen land," I guessed.

"Depends on where that easement is," Tobias said. "But that's the crux of the argument."

"Why don't the Nelsens just move where they're trying to build?" I asked.

"That would be losing the fight, admitting they were in the wrong, giving in," he said. "Plus the stone supports are already placed there. The farming Sorensens destroy the wood structure every time the Nelsens build a new bridge, but those stones remain. Like a dare."

"No one seems like the good guy the way you tell it," I said. Tobias just shrugged.

It took nearly half an hour for us to walk across the highway bridge and then down the bluff on the south side, and by the time we were once more in the river valley, the sun was fully risen over the lake. But that light wasn't going to last long. I could already see cloud cover rolling in from the west. We approached the steel bridge from the opposite direction than I had seen it the day before, but it still gleamed brightly in the first rays of dawn.

That sight only transfixed me for a split second, because the scene around the bridge was anything but tranquil. I could see my grand-mother standing with her back to me, a crowd of men and women between her and the bridge itself. The crowd was all talking at once, the voices loud and urgent but not shouty.

Not yet.

Most of the crowd had dark blond to light blond hair, like the two Sorensens who had come to fetch us, but a smaller group standing apart from the others had dark brown to black hair. I guessed those were the Nelsens, especially after I saw old Tore Nelsen standing among them. They were fewer, but if anything they were angrier. I guessed that was understandable, if the victim was one of them.

"Enough!" my grandmother suddenly commanded. Her voice carried over the furor, although she was not shouting. It sounded like a trick of the acoustics near the river, but I suspected she was adding a little magical oomph to it.

I thought that would be the end of the arguing, but to my surprise the Sorensens and Nelsens carried on bickering with each other. Tobias and I hurried our steps, but by the time we got there the fists were already flying.

"Mormor?" I said, both to let her know I was there and to ask her what I should do. She didn't so much as glance at me. She pressed a hand to her forehead, but only for a moment. Then she straightened up and threw both of her arms wide.

"Enough!" she said again, and her voice rang through the air like the bells warning of an attack by sea.

This time the fighting stopped, both among the people who were still arguing and the few who had decided to use violence to make their points. Fists were lowered, and everyone pulled apart to stand staring at their own feet like children caught making trouble.

But my grandmother didn't say anything to them. Then I saw that her knees were buckling, and I lunged to catch her before she could fall. She stayed on her feet, but her hands gripped my arms painfully tightly. Her breath was coming in hard pants like she'd just run some wind sprints.

"Mormor?" I asked.

"Too much," she said, mostly to herself. "Too much, too soon."

"Do you need my help?" I asked, although I had no idea what I could draw that would be of any use.

She held up a hand to me, and I fell silent. Then she turned to the others and just made a waving gesture. The crowd parted, and I helped her walk past them to the base of the bridge.

Then we saw the body. It was still in the water, floating face-down with some sort of spear in its back. It had hung up against the bridge support, but the way the current was tugging at it, I wasn't sure how much longer it would stay there.

The Konal could carry it out to the depths of Lake Superior in under a minute. I wondered if that had been the murderer's plan?

"We shouldn't touch it, right?" I whispered to my grandmother. "Look, we can see the weapon. Clearly this wasn't magic. And he's not a Villmarker. So we should leave this for the police. Right?"

"Yes, the police," my grandmother said as if half-asleep. But then she looked me straight in the eye and she was as wide awake and lucid as ever. "We need to be absolutely certain first. But, Ingrid, I don't think I'm up to this. Not today. Can you do it? Tell me true. If I leave you in charge, can you be absolutely sure that this isn't a matter for the two of us to deal with before the police arrive?"

"Yes, of course," I said. "I'll take a look around without disturbing anything and try to see if I sense anything. I've got this."

"Well, just do your best," she said, and my heart sank at her lack of faith in me. "Magic lingers. Once I've recovered, I can come back and look again. I'm not sensing anything now, but I'm not sure. And I want to be sure. I *need* to be sure. Do you understand?"

"Yes," I said. "I'll do my best."

"Good girl," she said, and tried to give me an encouraging smile. Mostly it just made me want to pick out a few of the bigger Sorensen farmers to carry her home. She looked dead on her feet.

But then she turned to the crowd and lifted her arms again to point at one then another of the troublemakers who had been fist-fighting moments before. "Listen, the police will be called, and they may have things to ask of you all. But for my part, I'm asking all of you to stay put. No one leaves Runde. Not until either this matter is resolved or I say otherwise. Understood?"

"Yes, Ms. Torfa," the oldest of the Sorensens said, shooting quelling looks at some of the younger Sorensens.

"Yes, Ms. Torfa," said an older woman who was standing among the Nelsens. Tore was close beside her, but not making eye contact with my grandmother. "I'll see my clan sits tight. But you swear to us you'll give us justice?"

"Don't I always?" my grandmother shot back, and the woman reluctantly nodded. "Good. Now, I have other things to attend to, but you will all give my granddaughter Ingrid all the assistance you would give me in her place. Ingrid, you're in charge."

Suddenly all eyes were on me, and I really wished the ground would just open up and swallow me. But it didn't. It just kept holding me up as my grandmother made her slow way back towards the path. But she didn't head back the way I'd come. She headed straight to the river. Did she know a shortcut? No one else seemed to notice, and in a moment she was gone from sight, lost behind the trees that grew near the riverbank.

And then I was alone, an outsider among two warring clans. And everyone was watching me closely, waiting to see what I'd do next.

CHAPTER 6

*T*he first thing I had to do was get rid of the audience. They were making me too self-conscious to even figure out where I should start. But how could I ask them all to leave? The eyes tracking my every move were deeply suspicious, Sorensen and Nelsen both.

"Andrew!" Tobias called suddenly, and I turned to see Andrew Swanson walking towards us, hands buried deep in his jeans pockets, the wind off the lake tossing the locks of his dark blond hair around. He looked up when he heard his name to give Tobias a wave, but then he saw me standing there next to Tobias and quickened his steps to join us.

"Ingrid," he said. His mouth kept twitching, and I gathered that he was suppressing a smile for me because of the gravity of the moment. "When did you get here?"

"Just a minute ago," I said. "You were already here, I take it?"

He nodded. "I just went to the Sorensen farmhouse to call the police from their landline. My cell wouldn't get any service down here by the creek."

"They're on their way?" I said, and he nodded again. "Not much time, then."

"Not much time for what?" he asked.

"My grandmother asked me to look around," I said. "Say, can you and Tobias convince these others to go home for now? They're not helping now, they didn't witness what happened then, and I'm sure the police will appreciate it if their crime scene isn't mobbed by citizens when they get here."

"Sure, we can do that," Andrew said. "But why are you looking around?"

"To set my grandmother's mind at ease," I said. "Another murder, you know?"

"Yeah, and they never solved the last one," Andrew said grimly. "Just be sure not to touch anything, right?"

"Of course," I said brightly. Then, as he and Tobias approached the others to convince them to move along, I turned to get my first close look at the body.

It was hard to tell much about the victim without touching anything. Facedown in the water with his water-logged jacket billowing around him, even saying it was a man was a bit of a guess. There was what looked like a spear in his back, but not a Villmarker spear, I didn't think. This was a modern tool, a fishing spear with three steel prongs. Which didn't mean that it couldn't be Villmarker; a lot of what they had up there was quite modern-looking. But I could see the manufacturer's logo on a sticker still stuck to the bottom of the wooden handle. Sometimes Villmarkers carved runes like a personal logo on their work, but they definitely never used stickers.

"What are you thinking?" Andrew asked. He had come over to stand beside me, and I glanced over to see Tobias walking away with the rest of his clan. The Nelsens were doing the same thing, but in a different direction. No one had crossed the bridge, though. The Sorensen farmhouse was further upstream, built close to the bank. I wasn't sure where the Nelsen place was, but the clan was heading east towards the lake.

"That's a fishing spear," I said. I didn't tell him that ruled out an entire village of potential suspects. He had no idea that Villmark even existed just a short walk away from where we were standing. Or that his best friend was a native of that place.

"That doesn't mean much," he said. I looked at him and raised an eyebrow. "I mean, it *could* have been a fishing Sorensen, but not necessarily. The professional fishermen in Runde all use nets, not spears. Some people spear fish, mostly in the river or streams and especially in this particular creek, but that could be anybody. It might not even have been a local. It could've been a tourist."

"Maybe," I conceded. He knew a lot more about what happened locally than I did. "But did he die from the stabbing or the drowning?"

"The police will figure that out," Andrew said, looking up as if to see if they were coming yet.

"They can get their cars down to this bridge, right?" I asked.

"Oh, sure," he said. "The bridge is between two farm fields, so that's just a tractor trail up there, but there's an old logging road that leads up to the farm on the west side. I sent Davey up to where that road meets the highway to flag them down so they don't get lost."

"You think of everything," I said. He just shrugged, but I could sense that suppressed smile again. "Did anyone figure out who he was yet? Tobias and Carl didn't know."

"Garrett Nelsen," Andrew said.

"You're sure?"

"The Nelsens were sure," he said. "I didn't know him well myself. He graduated the year before I started high school, and I never really saw him around town either. The Nelsens are pretty reclusive. Their kids don't really go in for extracurriculars."

"I noticed no one was throwing any accusations around when I got here," I said.

"No, this has taken everyone by surprise," Andrew said. "Garrett wasn't up to anything that could've led to this kind of trouble. Not that anyone in his family knew of, that is."

"So it wasn't about this bridge, then?" I asked. "I suppose it's possible he was stabbed further upstream and just got hung up here. Maybe at the Sorensen farm? Someone could've been hoping he'd float all the way to the lake."

"That's a lot of speculating," Andrew said.

"You're right," I said with a shrug. "Help me look around. Maybe we're missing some clues."

"Just to show the police when they get here," he said. "We're not touching anything."

"I know," I said. But as soon as I started looking around, I was immediately discouraged. "All the grass is flattened here, but the crowd we just dispersed probably did that themselves. I wish they would've stayed further back. Now there's no way to know if there was a fight here or not."

"I see something," Andrew said, pointing towards the muddy riverbank. I saw something there too, something that gleamed in a nonrock way. We both squatted down to examine the object.

"What is that?" I asked. "It's wood, but is it a little toy?"

"It looks like a whistle," he said, but I didn't see it. I shook my head in confusion. Then he raised a hand, indicating the length of it with a finger that came nowhere near touching the thing. "See, you blow in here, and the air and sound comes out here."

"Oh, sure," I said. "You said whistle, and I was picturing something round on one end like a coach's whistle or something. But this is more like a slide whistle without the slide. Or like a little flute."

"It's only going to make one note, and a bet it's a pretty irritating one. That's what kids like best. Luckily, I doubt it's so loud as a coach's whistle. But look, there's something written on it," he said, ducking his head closer to the ground. "It's mostly in the mud, but I definitely see the tops of something. Are those letters?"

"I see it too," I said. "But I can't tell what it says. Or how long it's been here. It might not actually be a clue at all."

"The police will decide," Andrew said, straightening up to look for approaching cars again.

"Maybe you should watch from the bridge," I suggested.

"Yeah," he said. "They should be here soon, but they might miss seeing us."

"I'm just going to take another look around and make sure we didn't miss anything," I said, then deliberately put my hands in the pockets of my windbreaker so he would know I wasn't going to touch things when he was gone. He nodded and started to climb the embankment, but a thought suddenly struck me. "Say, you haven't seen Luke around, have you?"

"Luke?" he repeated, stopping halfway up to look back at me. "No. Why?"

"No reason," I said. "I just wanted to ask him something."

"He doesn't usually come to this side of the river," Andrew said. "Is it important? Do you need me to call him? I usually have to leave him a message, but he always calls me back, usually inside of five minutes."

"No, it's not important," I said, indicating with a wave of my hand that he should continue on.

Once he was gone I turned my attention back to the river and the body within it. I sat down on the cold ground and slowed my breathing, reaching out with my magical senses the way my grandmother had been teaching me to.

But nothing happened. Except, after nearly five minutes of listening to the river burble by, I really needed a bathroom.

I was tempted to tell Andrew I had changed my mind, that he should call Luke. But I wouldn't be able to send a message to Luke through Andrew. First of all, he had no idea that Luke was really a Villmarker named Loke. Aside from that, I had no idea how to say "I need magical advice" in code.

I wished I had brought my bag with me with my sketchpad and pencils. Maybe if I drew what I saw, I would notice more. Not that I'd ever tried that before with magic, but I knew even in a mundane sense, I saw details in things when I was drawing them that I never noticed just looking at them. And drawing the waterfall parting had helped my grandmother the day before.

But I had left my bag at home.

I didn't sense anything magical, and certainly nothing seemed magical about a man who had been stabbed by a fishing spear and left to die in an icy cold creek on an October night.

But like my grandmother, I wanted to be *sure*, and I wasn't.

Because it was too possible that there was something there, but I didn't have the skills to perceive it.

I really wished Loke were there.

"They're coming!" Andrew leaned over the steel rail of the bridge to yell down at me.

"Great!" I called back, then scrambled up the embankment to meet him at the edge of the bridge. "You don't need me here, right? You can show the police everything without me."

"Sure," he said, but there was a quizzical arch to his brow.

"Like I said, my grandmother was worried and just wanted me to check things out," I said. "But she's not feeling too well, so I should really get back. If I'm here when the police arrive, who knows how long I could end up stuck here?"

"Yeah, no problem," he said. "Do you want me to stop by when I'm done here?"

"That would be great," I said. "You could fill mormor and me in on everything the police have to say. Thanks so much, Andrew."

"Not a problem," he said. "But you better take off." He pointed with his chin and I saw the first of the police cars coming around the bend behind me.

"Thanks!" I said, then slid back down the embankment to the river bank and jogged along the path back to the highway.

I really wished I knew what shortcut my grandmother had taken.

CHAPTER 7

$\mathcal{I}$ crossed the bridge back to the north side of the river, then followed the trail down the steep slope to the main road that ran through Runde. But once I was down there looking east towards my grandmother's house, I knew that wasn't really where I needed to be next. I didn't question the feeling, I just let it guide my steps past the meeting hall and up the river to the cavern behind the waterfall.

I had been here just the day before, but only a handful of times before that, and never without my grandmother. What was I thinking?

I straightened my spine and tried to put as much confidence as I could into my voice. "Which Thor is guarding?" I called, as mormor always did. I didn't think it was a coincidence it was always Thorbjorn when we'd come before. My grandmother clearly had a fondness for him. But who would it be this time?

Was I finally about to meet one of his brothers?

But there was no answer to my inquiry, and after a few minutes I started to feel a bit silly just waiting there. I went further in.

The passage to the inner caves was unblocked, and when I reached the fire cave, I found it empty. At first I thought the fire had gone out, but it was just banked down to a low glow of embers. There was plenty of wood nearby if someone wanted to build it back up to a roaring bonfire.

It was possible whoever was on guard duty was patrolling somewhere down in the deeper caves. But I would've thought they would block the passageway to Runde first.

The deeper caves, filled with things that mormor never spoke of and Thorbjorn only maddeningly hinted at. Was that passage also open and unguarded? Was that what had lured me here? Somewhere down there was the cave that was now Halldis' prison cell. And just that thought made my skin crawl, like I could feel her sensing my presence there in the cave. Like she knew I was alone, without mormor, without Thorbjorn.

I had a flash of a thought - what if I was following her summons again, like I had before? - and then found myself racing up the stone steps towards the meadow at the top of the waterfall, back up to the sunlight.

The image came back of her hands, those intricate motions. Was she somehow still casting spells?

Was she directly below me now?

That thought really had my heart racing, and by the time I reached the dry, brown grasses of the meadow at the top of the waterfall, I was in a full run. I didn't slow down until the houses of Villmark were all around me. Those modernist homes with their tidy little gardens surrounded me like a comforting hug, and I finally felt safe enough to slow down to a walk.

Safe, and a bit silly. I was behaving like a little girl, letting nightmares control me to the point I was jumping at every shadow. When my grandmother and I have a spare moment, I would ask her yet again about the safeguards she had placed to protect the Villmarkers from Halldis. I knew she had taken every precaution, and I had absolute faith that the power Halldis had was like a candle before the bonfire of what my grandmother could do.

But it wouldn't hurt to remind that scared part of my mind another time that we were safe now.

I walked to the center of town, nodding hello to the people I recognized or those who recognized me. It didn't seem like a large village, but I still had met all too few of the Villmarkers. The ones who went down to the meeting hall to mix with the people of Runde at least semiregularly were familiar to me, but there were many more that preferred to stay in their own village. Getting to know them was going to take more work from me. I should really make a point of doing that soon.

I took the north road from the center of town, climbing the hill until the road ended at its summit in a little park. The last house on my left was where the Thors lived. I knocked on the garden gate, but no one was in the garden. The morning chill was quickly burning off, promising another warm Indian summer day, although the clouds were drawing ever closer to the sun. I knocked again, louder, but there was still no response.

I had come too far to turn back now, even if I didn't really know why I was there besides having a feeling I was supposed to be there. Still, I felt like a complete criminal as I tried the gate latch and found it unlocked. I pushed the gate open, then hesitated.

My grandmother had a habit of just walking inside of any home in Villmark and Runde, both without waiting for an invitation, and no one ever seemed to mind. I suspected this was a measure of respect she commanded everywhere she went. But did that extend to me?

I was only crossing the yard, not breaking and entering, I reminded myself, and forced myself to walk up to the front door and knock on it. Then knock again. And a third time.

Maybe no one was home? I turned to look back towards the gate I had left standing open, but my feet wouldn't move. I needed to be here, but why?

I turned back to the door and reached for the doorknob, but a different impulse kept me from turning it. I just didn't have my grandmother's disregard for social niceties.

I don't know how long I stood there with my hand on the doorknob, caught between conflicting motivations, not able to move a muscle. But suddenly the door was thrown open with such force it tore the knob from my grip. I stumbled back, shaking my hand more in surprise than actual pain.

"Oh, Ingrid," Thorbjorn said. He tried to look up at me, but then shut his eyes against the sun behind me. "Come in." He didn't wait for me to respond, though, just grabbed my shoulder and propelled me inside so he could shut the door and block out the offending sunlight.

"You finished that whole huge mug of beer last night?" I guessed.

"That was only the first of many," he said. "I'll be right as rain as soon as I get some coffee and eggs in me, though. How about you?"

"I could use some of both," I admitted. "I've been up for a while but left the house in a hurry this morning. There's been a murder."

"Another one?" he said, still squinting when he looked at me like I was too bright for him.

"I think it's just a Runde matter," I said as I followed him down the hall to his family's kitchen. It featured a row of large floor-to-ceiling windows that offered an amazing view of the rest of the village on the hillside below. Luckily that view was aimed southerly and somewhat westerly, and the sun was a few hours away from reaching inside if the clouds didn't swallow it up first.

"Oh, good. My brothers left me some coffee," he said as he examined an immense stainless steel urn, the sort I associated with business meetings or church functions, places where a lot of people needed coffee all at the same time. All five Thors still lived with their parents, but even given that, it looked like a lot of coffee for seven people.

Thorbjorn filled a mug and set it on the kitchen table, gesturing for me to have a seat. I slid into the chair then put my face into the steam rising from the mouth of the mug, inhaling the aroma. I can take or leave the taste of coffee and generally prefer drinking tea, but there's nothing like the smell of roasted beans.

"You like it?" Thorbjorn asked as he filled a second mug for himself. "I can show you the shop where I get it in the marketplace. Nilda and Kara's aunt roasts the beans herself."

"It's not contraband here?" I asked.

"No, but the rules for getting that sort of thing are quite complicated," he said, taking a long swallow from his mug. "You can ask my dad about it sometime. He's the member of the council who mostly deals with trade issues."

"I have so much to learn," I said, taking a sip. I could see why he hadn't offered me any cream or sugar; the rich flavor needed no such adornments. "Wow."

Thorbjorn tried to grin at me but couldn't quite manage it. "Eggs?" he asked.

"Do you want me to-" I started to say, but he put a hand on my shoulder before I could get up from my chair.

"Absolutely not," he said. "This is not my first hangover, thank you very much."

"I wouldn't have thought so," I said. "I'm guessing the arm wrestling went on for a bit after I left?"

"There were... other events as well," he said as he took an enormous cast-iron skillet down from a hook and gave it a showy spin in one hand before setting it down on the stove. He had to use a match to light the burner, but in most respects the stove worked just like a modern one, if as oversized for a single family as the coffee urn was. He left it to heat up and started cracking egg after egg into a stainless steel bowl.

"Your brothers got up earlier than you?" I asked as I watched him crumble sausage into the skillet. I could smell fennel and garlic in addition to the meat.

"The ones who came home at all," he said. "Two of them were on forest patrol. It's not unusual for that to mean being out for a few nights at a time."

I sensed he wanted to wait until he had food in him before conducting any serious conversation, so I just sipped at my coffee and watched him brown the sausage then pour in the eggs. A few minutes after that he finally set a plate of scrambled eggs and sausage in front of me, then sat down across from me with his own.

At first he ate without speaking, forking mouthful after mouthful without interruption in a studious rhythm. But then finally he paused to take another gulp of coffee and looked up at me.

To my surprise, he seemed to be totally right about just needing coffee and breakfast to be right as rain. His eyes were clear and alert, as if he had just gotten a full night's sleep after a quiet evening at home. "You said something about a murder?" he said.

"Like I said, it's probably just a Runde matter. And the police are already working on it," I said.

"But that's why you were up so early this morning, I'm guessing," he said between bites.

"Mormor and I both, yes," I said. "The body was found under the new steel bridge. You know the one. We sailed past it yesterday?"

"Sure," he said. "I regret my words."

"What words?" I asked.

"When I told you about the build and destroy cycle of the bridge there, and I said steel was going to make things interesting. No, what I said was, it would be *fun* to see what happened next. I didn't think it would be murder."

"I'm not sure this is related to that," I said. "He might not have even been killed there. We can't tell."

"Just a weird coincidence?" he asked.

"I don't know. Maybe it is related in some way. Since the dead body was a Nelsen, and the kid who found him was a Sorensen, and those are the two families that have been having a property dispute over that bridge since the founding of Runde."

"I can't help you with that," he said. "In fact, I don't know what I *can* help you with. Besides breakfast."

"Yeah, thanks for that," I said, looking down at my empty plate. I had been hungrier than I had thought.

"Did you come here just because you were hungry?" he asked.

"I don't know why I came here," I admitted. "I was going back to my grandmother's house after the police arrived to take over the crime scene, but instead I found myself walking here. I just felt like there was something I needed to do here."

"In Villmark, or in my house?" he asked. I shrugged. Then he gave me a sharp look. "Wait, you came up here alone? Not with your grandmother?"

"No, she's still recovering from yesterday," I said. "Are you angry with me? You look angry."

"I'm not angry with you," he said. "I should've felt you crossing from Runde to Villmark and I didn't."

"Well," I said, but couldn't think of a diplomatic way of pointing out his hangover, or the fact that I had obviously woken him up when I had knocked on the door. "Look, I know it sounds crazy, letting some random urge out of nowhere dictate what I do."

"Not at all," he said with a wave of his hand. "You don't have full access to your magic yet, but that doesn't mean it isn't trying to communicate with you anyway it can. I think trusting your urges is the smart play." Then he got up from the table and gathered our plates to take them over to the deep sink already filled with soaking dishes.

"Do you need help washing up?" I asked.

"I don't think that's why you were summoned here," he said, but before either of us could say more we were interrupted by a knock at the door. "Although you can help by seeing who that is," he said.

"Sure," I said, and went back up the hallway to open the front door.

It was Loke. And he didn't look surprised to see me in Thorbjorn's house.

"Loke," I said. "Thorbjorn is just in the kitchen."

"I'm sure he is, but I'm actually here for you," he said with a sly grin.

"Me? How did you even know I was here?" I asked.

"Well, where else would you be at this hour?" he asked, but then raised his hands as if in defense when I narrowed my eyes at him. "Also, Mjolner is waiting at the gate. That's usually a dead giveaway."

"Mjolner is here?" I asked, leaning around Loke to see that my cat was indeed sitting on top of the gatepost, calmly grooming his sleek black ears.

"That's not the important bit," Loke said. "You better bid your farewells to Thorbjorn. Andrew is at your grandmother's house."

"Why does that sound dire?" I asked, narrowing my eyes at him again.

"I don't know," he said with a careless shrug. "People tend to think everything I say sounds dire. I don't intend it. All I know is Andrew is at your grandmother's house, and she flagged me down as I passed on the street to send me here to fetch you."

"She knew I was in Villmark?" I asked.

"Mjolner probably tipped her off," he said.

"But what does Andrew want?" I asked. "Did the police find out something?"

"Police?" Loke said, raising his eyebrows with a questioning air that I didn't think he was faking. "Sorry. I was given orders, not information. The only way to find out is to go back home."

"Right," I said, and held up a finger to tell him to wait for me as I headed back to the kitchen to say goodbye to Thorbjorn.

I still had no clue why my gut had sent me here, but I wasn't having any luck figuring out what it was, and the person who could help me most was my grandmother. So I might as well head home.

But I couldn't quiet the nagging feeling that I was missing something.

CHAPTER 8

$\mathcal{I}$ gave Loke a rundown of my entire morning as we walked back to my grandmother's house. He listened intently without interrupting, but drew me to a halt just before we climbed up onto the porch.

"This urge to see Thorbjorn," he said. I expected to see his eyes dancing at me, but he looked, for once, completely serious. "What was that?"

"I don't know," I said. Mjolner was squirming in my arms and I bent to let him go run through the dried remains of the herb garden.

"Come on. Do better than that," he scoffed. "You've been under a compulsion spell, right? You've also followed magical feelings before. Was this like either of those?"

"Maybe like the second one?" I said.

"You don't sound sure," he said.

"Maybe because I'm not sure," I said. "The feeling was strong as I went to Villmark, but as soon as I got there, it just sort of faded away."

"I thought it led you all the way to Thorbjorn's house," he said. "Ingy, think carefully. Were you guided the whole way?"

"Don't call me Ingy," I said, but when he put his hand over my eyes, I let him close my eyelids, and I thought back to what I had been feeling but not really paying attention to before. "No. The feeling sort of tapered off, and I guess I figured as long as I was there I would go see Thorbjorn."

"I thought so," he said, and I opened my eyes to see him smirking.

"That's not helpful," I said.

"Sorry, helpful is not really my thing," he said with his trademark casual shrug. "But seriously, when you get these feelings in the future, take more note of them."

"I guess I didn't realize I wasn't," I said. "But thanks for the advice. Shall we?"

He nodded, and I skipped up the steps. The moment I swung the door open, the smell of fresh waffles, butter and real maple syrup washed over me.

"There she is," Andrew said, or tried to say. The waffle packed in his mouth muffled his words.

"Here I am," I agreed, getting out of my boots as quickly as I could and running to take over the waffle iron.

"I've got this," my grandmother tried to insist, but Loke was already there beside her, guiding her to a chair. It was a sign of just how exhausted she was that she let him do that.

"Nora? Are you not feeling all right?" Andrew asked. He looked guiltily down at his syrupy plate, now empty of waffles.

"Oh, yes," she assured him. "I just had a bit of a full day yesterday."

"And an early morning," he said. "I should not have sent Carl and Tobias to wake you."

"Nonsense. I needed to know," she said. The waffle light went from red to green and I lifted the lid, then forked the hot waffle onto an empty plate. I handed it to Loke, who set it in front of my grandmother.

"So Luke said you needed me back straight away?" I said as I poured another ladle-full of batter onto the iron and closed the lid.

"Yes, things have gotten a little complicated while you were away," my grandmother said, not touching the waffle in front of her. I gave Loke a pointed look, and he slipped into the empty chair beside her to start buttering it for her.

"I haven't been gone long," I said, then glanced at my watch and realized it had been more than an hour.

"Where were you?" Andrew asked.

"I took a walk. I needed to think," I said. "What's happened? Did the police say something?"

"No, not to me," Andrew said. "They chased me out of there as soon as they arrived. But one of the junior officers, a fellow named Foster, told me they would keep the Nelsen family informed of the investigation as it proceeds. So that's something."

I remembered Officer Foster. He had had a pretty tough time the last time he had come to Runde. My grandmother maintained some sort of magic that made people either not notice Runde or to forget it the moment they left. He had come down to Runde proper to question me but had had trouble remembering who my grandmother and I were from moment to moment even as he was talking to us. But then, he had been in the meeting hall when he had tried to question me about Lisa's death. That was the very heart of my grandmother's protective spells. I hoped he had fared better on the far side of the river.

"Are you friends with any of the Nelsens?" I asked. "Anyone who would share any information with us?"

"Not really," Andrew said.

"Tore will come to me," my grandmother said. "Whether the news is good or bad, he'll come tell me."

"Well, that's something," I said. "But if we're just waiting to hear something, why send Luke to fetch me?"

"We're not all waiting, apparently," my grandmother said, then rolled up the waffle on her plate and began eating from one end like it was a buttery burrito.

"What does that mean?" I asked.

"Two of the Sorensens are gone," Andrew told me. "Maybe it doesn't mean anything-"

"Or maybe they're guilty," I finished for him.

"They left after I told them all to stay," my grandmother said, and her eyes were boring into mine, looking for a sign that I understood what she was really saying.

"They were there this morning, when you told everyone to stay?" I guessed. She nodded, satisfied that I had caught her meaning, and turned her attention back to her waffle.

I had thought my grandmother had been using magic to amplify her voice, but now I was pretty sure she had put a little compulsion in it as well, to get the others to do as she asked. That made sense. She had been so quickly drained by what she did, it had to be more magically taxing than just making her voice sound louder.

"Are we suspicious?" Loke asked. His eyes were moving from me to my grandmother, but it was Andrew who answered.

"It doesn't look great," he said as he got up to carry his plate to the sink. "Why would they leave in such a hurry?"

"Who left?" I asked.

"Keith and Ralf, two cousins about my age," Andrew said. "They're both farming Sorensens. Carl told me they were going to their hunting cabin. They hadn't bagged anything yet, and the season ends tomorrow."

"Haven't bagged any what yet?" I asked. "What are they hunting?"

"Bear," he said. "Their story checks out as far as it goes. The bear season ends tomorrow, and if they had gotten one already, it would be the talk of the town."

Then he turned on the water and started scrubbing the sticky syrup off of his plate. My grandmother quickly waved for Loke and I to lean in closer to her.

"Do you think they've gotten into something magical that let them circumvent your orders?" Loke asked in a hurried whisper.

"Sadly, I don't think so. I think I'm just that off my game these days," my grandmother said. Then she turned to me. "Villmark?"

"I was compelled to," I said, and I could feel my cheeks flushing guiltily.

"Not an outside force," Loke quickly added. "But if it was a guiding force, it was a vague one." My grandmother nodded at his words as if they made sense to her.

"What are we talking about?" I asked.

"Yes, what are we talking about?" Andrew asked as well as he turned off the water and reached for the dishtowel to dry his hands.

"We should go find those two Sorensens," Loke said.

"We? You mean us?" Andrew asked.

"Luke and I can do it," I said.

"No, I'm not trying to get out of helping," he said. "Most of my day is free, so I'm all yours. It's just, isn't this a police matter?"

"Do the police think they are suspects?" Loke asked, raising his eyebrows.

"I have no idea. Do *we* think they're suspects?" Andrew countered.

"Anyone could get a hold of a fishing spear," I mumbled to myself, but when I noticed everyone was leaning in to hear me, I went on at a normal volume. "They left when my grandmother specifically asked them not to. You thought that was important enough to come tell us."

"Yeah," Andrew said, rubbing the back of his neck. He looked confused, like he didn't know why he had done that.

"We should just talk to them," Loke said. "Maybe they really did go to hunt bear, and we can just give them a talking to for not checking in before they left town. Or maybe there's a different reason they left." Andrew was still rubbing at his neck, but Loke caught my eye and tapped his own sternum. At first I didn't understand, but then I realized he was touching the point just below the V in his sweater's neck. The point where he could hide an amulet, as Halldis had hidden hers.

I raised my eyebrows at him. *These two Runde brothers had access to magic like that?*

Loke just shrugged. *Who knows?*

"Yes, we should talk to them," I agreed, out loud for Andrew's benefit. "I haven't taken my car out for a spin since Andrew's dad finished fixing it up. Assuming we know where to find them?"

"I can get the address from Tobias," Andrew said, reaching for the phone in his back pocket.

"Great," Loke said, pushing up from the table and making a show of stretching out his back. "It's a tiny car, isn't it?"

"It's a Volkswagen Beetle," I said. "You don't have to come-"

"Oh, I'm coming," he said. "I'm curious about this business."

"I'll come too," Andrew said absentmindedly, his thumbs still typing out a text.

"And Mjolner and I shall stay here," my grandmother said, shoving the cat in question off the table before he could get a paw into the open crock of butter. As usual, he had gotten from the yard into the house without the aid of a cat door. "I think I'll take a little bit of a nap. But, Ingrid, be sure to wake me the minute you get back to Runde. No wandering off."

"Yes, mormor," I promised, fighting the urge to raise my fingers in the scout's gesture.

"I mean it," she said, but her voice lacked force. She looked really tired, and I was tempted to send Andrew and Loke to investigate without me. But then she looked up at me again. "Wake me when you get back. We have some other matters to discuss, but for now I need sleep."

I promised again, secretly hoping that the next time we were both at the table together, we'd be alone.

CHAPTER 9

$\mathcal{A}$lthough the repairs - the very extensive, very expensive repairs - had been completed more than a week ago, my car was still in Andrew's father's garage behind the gas station. There really wasn't anywhere to park it at my grandmother's house. So after leaving the house, we had to climb the steep path up the bluff to the level of the highway.

This was the fourth time I'd hiked uphill that day, and it was barely past breakfast time. But that was no longer unusual for me these days. Without intending to, I was getting into much better shape than I'd been in since I'd left my high school track days behind. I no longer got more than mildly winded, although I was still in awe of my grandmother, who had twice my stamina at more than three times my age.

"You've started it up, right?" Andrew asked as we emerged at the top of the path and headed across the overly large, empty parking lot to the open doorway to his father's garage. "You know it runs?"

"Your dad had me do that when he was done fixing it," I said. "It starts fine."

"But you didn't drive it around?" he asked.

"No," I confessed. "I meant to take it out some Sunday, maybe drive down to Duluth, but stuff kept coming up." I knew that sounded lame to his ears. He didn't know about my intensive course of magical study, and I couldn't really think of another excuse for being busy all the time when he knew I didn't have a job.

"I suppose," Andrew said. "Jessica told me you're going to be hanging some of your work up in her café. That's cool. You're getting your name out there."

"Yes, although it's past tourist season, so I'm not getting my hopes up just yet," I said.

"It'll be skiing season before you know it," he said. "We get traffic then too. I know Jessica is hoping to capitalize on that since she opened too late for summer tourists."

"I should probably get some stuff framed then," I said, more to myself than to him.

We went inside the garage and I saw my parents' little yellow Volkswagen Beetle waiting for me just where I'd left it. It didn't look as good as new, but it didn't look like I'd driven it straight into a tree either.

"Finally taking her out?" Andrew's father Jens asked. It took a second for me to find where he was, but then he slid out from under another car and sat up, wiping his greasy hands on an equally greasy rag.

"Yes," I said. "We're heading up the Gunflint Trail a ways."

"Well, go ahead and start her up again," he said, tucking the rag into the pocket of his coveralls. "I want to give her another listen before I let you go."

"Okay," I said, sliding into the driver's seat. Andrew got into the passenger side, and Loke somehow managed to fold up his long legs enough to slide past the driver's seat to fit in the tiny backseat.

I suspected magic may have been involved.

Then I pushed the seat back and got in. I put the key in the ignition and held my breath before giving it a turn. The engine roared instantly to life, but something was wrong. I couldn't quite place it, but it didn't sound like it should.

"Sounds good," Jens said, then looked at me. "You don't think so?"

"I don't know," I said. "Something's off."

"Tell me," he said. "I always listen to a driver's instincts."

"I don't think I have a driver's instinct," I said, but suddenly I knew what was wrong. "The rattle. It's gone."

"Well, yeah," he said. "Did you want to keep it?"

"No, this is great," I said. "I don't think I've ever heard this engine run so smooth."

"Well, if you do run into any trouble, you have Andrew there with you," Jens said, rubbing his hands on the rag again. He wasn't getting them any cleaner. "He has the skill of a mechanic, if not the calling. Failing that, call me. I can come get you with the tow truck."

"Thanks, Mr. Swanson," I said.

"It's Jens," he said, gesturing towards the highway, or more correctly towards the gas station that stood between us and it. "Mr. Swanson is my father."

"Thank you, Jens," I said. I hadn't met the eldest Swanson, not having gone inside the gas station yet, but I had seen him through the windows when I was walking by, and he always gave me a wave.

I backed out of the garage and then pulled up to the freeway. As I was checking for traffic, I saw that Andrew was slumped down in his seat, arms crossed and a rather grumpy look on his face. I waited until I was safely up to speed on the highway before asking, "what's up?"

"She means with you, dummy," Loke said, nudging Andrew in the shoulder when he didn't answer my question.

"I'm fine," he said. "It's just that thing with my dad."

"What thing with your dad?" I asked.

"The thing where he's always on about how I don't want to do my part in the family business."

"I must've missed that thing," I said. I caught Loke's eye in my rearview mirror, but he just shrugged. "Your dad seemed pretty understanding, in as much as he even mentioned it."

"It sounds different to a practiced ear," Andrew said.

"He said you had skill," I said.

"With engines," Andrew said.

"Isn't that still a good thing?" I asked.

61

"As far as that goes, sure," he said grumpily. "He's never going to say I have skill with any other line of work. That's the point."

"Oh, that's the point?" Loke said, amusing himself if not the rest of us.

"But we were talking about cars," I said. "What else was he supposed to say?"

"Never mind," Andrew said, and sank lower into his seat.

"Artists," Loke said. "So temperamental."

"Hey," I said. "*I'm* not temperamental."

"Whatever," Loke scoffed. "I've heard you lamenting to Michelle and Jessica that you haven't sold anything yet. It's only been a month since you got here. Being impatient is a temperament."

I decided not to respond to that. But it wasn't easy. "So, what are these two Sorensens like?" I asked. "Do you know them?"

"They're cousins, both farming Sorensens," Andrew said, and finally started to untense his body. "Keith and Ralf. I knew them a little in high school. They were both two years ahead of me. They really like to hunt."

"I don't suppose you know if either of them ever go spear fishing?" I asked.

"It's possible," he said.

"Do you think they're the type to be angry about that bridge?" I asked.

"Definitely yes," he said. "If there was ever a fight at school, it was nearly always between a farming Sorensen and a Nelsen. And Keith and Ralf were involved as much as anybody. But murder? I don't know. It just seems so... extreme."

"It is, no matter who did it," Loke said from the back seat. "Do you know how hard it would be to kill someone like that? The prongs wouldn't do it, not unless you nicked something vital by some fluke. No, you'd pretty much have to hold them underwater until it was done."

"That's grim," I said.

"You'd almost have to have a deep sustained anger to do it," he said. "That's our suspect list. Angry people."

We reached Grand Marais, and I turned off the highway at the sign shaped like a voyageur portaging his canoe, the words Gunflint Trail spelled out on the side of his canoe. We soon left signs of civilization behind as the road ran through the hills and past the lakes of the Superior National Forest.

I would really have to come back sometime with my sketchbook. The views were as inspiring as any Viking ship.

Well, almost.

"It's just on the other side of this lake," Andrew said after we'd passed the better part of an hour in silence. "There's an unmarked road, easy to miss. That's what Tobias told me."

"I'll slow down," I said, glancing in my rearview to be sure no one was behind me before letting off the gas. We reached the other side of the lake at a crawl and had no trouble making the turn, although I could see why Tobias had said it would be easy to miss. Weeds nearly overran the dirt road, and the trees were so close on either side it felt tight even in the Volkswagen.

We bumped and rolled over the potholed road until finally a little cabin came into view. The road led up to it and ended in a little turn-about between the cabin and what appeared to be an outhouse. I pulled up next to a pickup truck and shut off the engine.

"Wake up, Luke," Andrew said, reaching into the back seat to give Loke a swat on the knee. He opened just one eye to glare at Andrew.

"I'm awake," he said. "Are they here?"

"That's what we're about to find out," Andrew said.

I got out of the car and stretched out my back as I looked around. The cabin was in the middle of a forest of evergreen trees with the occasional stand of now leafless birch. The only sound was the ticking of my engine as it cooled.

Andrew and then Loke got out of the other side of the car and the three of us walked up to the cabin to knock on the door, but there was no answer.

"Outhouse, maybe?" I said.

"There's another shed in back," Loke said. "I'm going to check it out."

But there was no one in the outhouse or the shed, and no one answered a knock at the back door either.

"Well, if they really came here to hunt-" I said.

"They'd be out in the woods," Andrew finished for me with a sigh. "Hopefully they don't range far from the cabin." But he didn't sound hopeful.

"We should split up," Loke said. He pointed to the thickest patch of woods behind the cabin, "Andrew, you go that way. Ingy, you take the strip of trees between here and the road. I'll take everything between."

"I have two bars," Andrew said, looking at his phone. "Better than none, which is what we'll probably have away from the cabin. We should meet back here in an hour whether we find anyone or not. Agreed?"

"Agreed," I said, and started towards my assigned area, but very slowly. The minute Andrew disappeared into the trees, I ran to catch Loke before he was out of sight. "Loke, can we do anything?"

"We are doing something," he said with the usual perverse humor in his voice.

"I meant something magical, something to speed this up," I said.

"Speeding up is good," he said. "But magic out here is less so."

"What do you mean?" I asked.

He gave an exaggerated sigh. "Haven't you been learning *anything* about magic yet?"

"Yes, but for the sake of argument, let's say no," I said. "Just tell me what you mean."

"Look, for now it's best if you don't try to do anything outside of Runde," he said. "And of course Villmark is safer."

"Why?" I asked. "Is it going to blow up in my face, or attract other magic-users, or what?"

"All the above," he said. "Just don't. And ask your mormor about it. She's going to want you to have her answer to that, not mine."

"Not yours because you totally do magic wherever you want to, don't you?" I asked. I could hear mischief in my own voice. He was rubbing off on me.

His eyes glinted with manic glee, but he kept his voice stern.

"Never you mind about that. You have a job to do. That's your section over there."

"I'm going, I'm going," I said.

I headed into my section of the woods, which was more beech than evergreen. This made it easier going, the branches spread wide overhead as I shuffled through the piles of dried leaves. I could occasionally catch glimpses of another lake up ahead of me, which was good. If I was searching a box between the road and the cabin with lakes on the other two sides, I couldn't get lost.

The moment that thought struck me, I realized I couldn't hear just where the road was. There had only been occasional traffic when we'd been driving on it, but I should be hearing cars pass every couple of minutes, and I wasn't. I turned towards where I thought the road should be, but there was no sign of it through the trees.

I looked at my phone. I had no bars, and most of the hour had passed while I had been in a daydream of admiring the trees with their patterned bark and delicate limbs. I should head back.

I turned again and started walking the way I had come. Only nothing was looking familiar. But there had been no real landmarks on the walk out, just tree after tree. I hadn't paid enough attention to the forest while looking at the trees to be sure this wasn't the way I had come. The sky overhead was completely cloudy now, the sun obscured and no help.

Then I saw something in the trees ahead of me. Not anything familiar, but something that meant civilization: a hunting stand. I climbed up to peek at the platform, but if it had been used recently or not, I had no way of knowing. Still, I had to be getting closer to the cabin.

Didn't I?

"Hello?" I called, just in case one of the Sorensens was anywhere near the hunting stand. No one answered, but I did hear something like a twig snapping. I turned towards the sound and started walking.

"Hello?" I called again. "Is anyone there?"

I kept walking, my feet making shushing noises through the thick bed of dried leaves. I peered through the trees ahead of me and was just thinking that I could see the yard behind the cabin. Wasn't that the shed there between those two trees?

Then I stepped down on a branch I hadn't seen under the leaf cover, and it snapped under my foot with a loud crack.

Things got confusing after that. Something moved ahead of me, but it was not so much like a thing in the woods was turning as the woods itself was turning to confront me.

And it had a rifle. That part I was absolutely sure about.

CHAPTER 10

Someone screamed. I think it was me.

Then the end of the rifle that had been all too near my face fell away.

"Oh my god, I'm so sorry," someone said, but I was still having a hard time focusing. I had never stared down the barrel of a gun before. It wasn't a pleasant experience. "I'm so sorry. Are you okay?"

"Am I?" I asked, looking down at my own hands as if they contained the answer. I didn't appear to be shot.

"You startled me," the man said, and I finally looked up at him. He was wearing a camouflage suit, and as my eyes moved up to his face, he pushed back the hood that had been covering his head. "That's not an excuse. I was jumpy. This is totally on me. Are you okay?"

"I'm okay," I assured him, finally able to get my own mind calmed. "Are you Keith or Ralf?"

"Keith," he said, sounding surprised. "Do I know you?"

"I'm Ingrid Torfa," I said.

"Oh," he said, blinking. And then his face flushed a deep red. "Oh. We're in trouble, aren't we?"

"That depends on what you did," I said. "Where's your cousin?"

"He's around here somewhere," Keith said. Then he deepened his voice so it would carry and shouted, "Ralf!"

"Andrew Swanson and Luke are waiting for me at the cabin," I said, stumbling a bit when I said Luke's name. I had no idea what last name he used in Runde, or even what his family name might be up in Villmark.

"Right. It's this way," he said, slinging his rifle over his back and reaching for my elbow to guide me through the trees.

So I hadn't been looking at the shed just then. Perhaps it had been a good thing I had run into him when I had. But I could've wished for better circumstances.

"I don't know how I could've sneaked up on you," I said. "There are a lot of leaves on the ground, and I wasn't exactly trying to be quiet."

"I know. I am sorry," he said again. "I think I might've fallen asleep there for a little bit. I was in like a fugue state. You know?"

"Actually, I do," I said, although in my mind a fugue state meant magic. I doubted that was what he meant, though.

Or rather, I hoped that wasn't what he meant.

We had just emerged from the woods and were crossing the cabin's backyard when Loke and Andrew burst out of the trees at a run.

"There she is!" Loke said and stopped running to put his hands on his knees and get his breath back.

"What happened?" Andrew demanded, looking from me to Keith and back again. "We heard you scream."

"I just got startled," I said.

"That was a pretty sustained scream for being startled," he said.

"It was my fault," Keith said. "She startled me."

"*You* screamed?" Loke asked.

"No," Keith said. He took a breath to explain but his cheeks started to flush and I turned to see what had to be his cousin Ralf coming up the road. He looked at Loke still fighting to get his breath back, then at Andrew and I and finally at Keith, noting how his cousin was blushing and not meeting his eyes.

"What happened?" he demanded.

"I don't know," Keith stammered. "I was alone, and then something was right behind me, like right behind me. Like it was towering over me, right? But when I spun around, it was just Ingrid here." And then his cheeks flushed even darker.

"I don't understand that story," Ralf said.

"Neither do I and I was there," I said.

"You're the one who screamed?" he asked.

"Yeah, but in my defense, I thought he was going to shoot me," I said.

Keith raised his hands in surrender, then flinched when his cousin gave him a hard glare.

"He pointed his gun at you?" Andrew asked.

"I don't think he meant to," I said, but despite my words the mood in the air darkened another couple of degrees.

"I'm sorry," Keith said again, apparently to all of us.

Ralf continued to glare at his cousin for another moment, but then turned to me and Andrew. "I guess I know why you're here. We should go inside."

"Lead the way," Andrew said. Ralf nodded, then headed towards the cabin's back door. The interior was all one room, with bunk beds near a gigantic stone fireplace and a few tables and chairs scattered about the rest of the space.

"Coffee?" Ralf offered as he gestured for us to take the chairs closest to the cold fireplace.

"Sounds good," I said, flopping down onto one of the chairs.

"Are you okay?" Andrew whispered to me the moment Ralf and Keith stepped away from us to put their guns away.

"I'm fine," I said, hoping he wouldn't press. I wanted to hear what the Sorensens were saying to each other. But they didn't seem to be making any last-minute effort to get their stories straight or craft an alibi or anything.

No, from the few words I could catch, Ralf was lecturing Keith on firearm safety and an embarrassed Keith was just nodding over and over again. At least he wasn't making any excuses. But he wasn't offering an explanation either.

"I can't believe he did that," Andrew whispered as if reading my mind.

"He said he was in a fugue state," I whispered back, but that was really meant for Loke's ears. If he heard me, he made no sign.

"No excuse," Andrew grumbled. He looked up as Ralf came to sit with us.

"Your grandmother sent you, I'm guessing?" he said as he pulled the wool cap from his head and gave his flattened hair a vigorous rub.

"You were told not to leave town," Andrew said.

"It was a request," I said. "Not an order."

"That was how I understood it," Ralf said.

"Semantics," Loke scoffed. "It doesn't matter how it was phrased or how you understood it. You better have a good reason to disobey Nora Torfa." Then he got up from his chair and started pacing the scant space in front of the fireplace. "We should put them in separate rooms to question them."

"Separate rooms?" Ralf asked.

"There's just the one room, Luke," I pointed out.

"But why?" Ralf asked. "So we left Runde to come here. We had every right to. Why would you need to question us in separate rooms about that? We're scarcely going to lie about it."

"That's not all we're talking about and you know it," Loke said.

Ralf glowered at him. I leaned forward to speak, to say something to put Ralf at ease, but Loke shot me the briefest of looks and gave his head the smallest of shakes. I sat back without saying a word.

"We have no intention of lying," Ralf said again. He glanced up at Keith as he approached with mugs of instant coffee in his hands, and Keith nodded his agreement.

"Lying about what?" Andrew asked.

"Last night," Ralf said. "That's what you came here to ask us about, right? Not that you were there. But she was."

I realized he meant me. But the only place I'd been the night before that Ralf would know about was the meeting hall. Had he also been there?

Then I remembered that I had seen him, him and Keith both. They had been at the table in the corner when all the Villmarkers had arrived after the day out on the lake. The table where Roarr had later sat.

"Are you confessing?" Andrew asked, confused.

"No," Ralf said. "We didn't do anything. We were just talking about it."

"Well," Keith said, but tapered off without saying anything more.

"Fine," Ralf grumbled. "More than talking. Planning. But what does it matter? We never *did* anything."

"Nothing but plan a murder?" Andrew asked.

Ralf choked on his coffee. "Murder?"

"That's why we're here," I said. "Garrett Nelsen. You were there this morning. No point in pretending this is news to you."

"No, we were there," he admitted. "But we had nothing to do with that."

"I'm confused," Andrew said, pressing his hands to his face.

But I thought I knew what was going on. "You were planning something last night," I said. "At the meeting hall, the two of you with I'm guessing some others? Not a murder, but some other mischief. Probably something to do with that new bridge."

The two Sorensens traded a glance, and I knew I had guessed correctly.

"But like you said, you didn't do it," I said. "The bridge is still there, same as yesterday. So why run?"

"We're innocent in the eyes of the law," Ralf said. "But your grandmother is a different thing."

"She'd know," Keith said. "Just by looking at us, she'd know what we were planning to do. She always knows."

"So you ran away to avoid my grandmother giving you a stern talking to?" I asked.

Loke leaned over my shoulder to whisper in my ear, but it was a stage whisper designed to carry. "I'd run."

"We didn't have anything to do with the murder," Ralf said. "We didn't see anything that could help, either. There was no reason for us to stay."

"We were drinking," Keith said.

"In the meeting hall when you made your bridge-destroying plans," I said.

"And after," Keith said. "We were going from barn to barn looking for anything that would burn. Kerosene or something."

"It wasn't a particularly well-formed plan," Ralf said. "More just an impulse. I don't think any of us thought we'd actually do it."

"I did," Keith said, but barely more than a whisper. "I thought we would. But somehow we ended up doing more drinking than searching in the third barn we went to. Then we woke up there when the others were all running past the barn to get to the creek."

"We blended in with the crowd," Ralf said. "If you asked them, most of them would probably tell you we were with them all night. I'm not sure anyone realized we weren't."

"If you thought you had an alibi, why did you run?" Andrew asked. "I mean, you said you didn't even commit the crime you started out doing, and no one suspects you of the actual crime. Your actions don't make a lot of sense."

"They really don't," Keith agreed, but fell silent at his cousin's glare.

"Maybe they do," I said. Loke nodded from where he now stood behind Andrew. But Andrew just looked confused. I stood up. "Sorensens, wait here. We three are going to step outside for a moment." I waved for Loke and Andrew to follow me. I lead the way outside, then stopped a few feet away from the door. "Thoughts?" I asked.

"They're screwy," Andrew said. "Nothing they said makes any sense."

"Maybe it doesn't matter," I said. "If they didn't commit the murder, anything else they may or may not have been up to really isn't our business. And I don't think they were involved in the murder. As strange as their story is, I believe the gist of what they're saying."

"I guess I do too," Andrew said. "If they had killed someone last night, I don't think they would've invited us in to talk about it over instant coffee. No, they don't seem guilty."

"I agree, so far as that goes," Loke said.

"Great," I said with a sigh. "Kind of a waste of a morning, but whatever. Andrew, can you go inside and tell them to pack up? We're going to follow them back to Runde."

Andrew nodded and walked back to the house.

"Fugue state," Loke said the minute I turned to him.

"We're thinking the same thing," I said.

"Maybe," he said. "On the other hand, if they really were drinking all day yesterday..." He trailed off with his hands in the air, but I could follow his thoughts from there.

"Yeah, maybe it's just part of his hangover," I said. "Still, something is bothering me."

"What's that?" he asked.

But we were interrupted by Andrew's return, Ralf and Keith close behind him. I watched as they put their guns and duffle bags in the back of the truck.

"Sorensens, I have a question," I said.

"Just one?" Ralf asked.

"For now," I said. "You weren't acting alone last night. But you've been careful not to name names. Do you mind telling me who else was part of your bridge-burning party? Another Sorensen, perhaps?"

"No, it wasn't," Ralf said. "Actually, I don't think I know his full name." He shot a look at Keith, who shrugged. "No, no idea. He's just a drinking buddy, usually. This was the first time we'd ever been anywhere with him besides the meeting hall."

"Was his name Roarr, by any chance?" Loke asked.

"Yeah, that's it," Keith said. "I don't know if that's a first name, a last name, a nickname or what. But he looks like he probably played football back in his day."

"Followup question," I said. "Was it his idea that the two of you take off this morning?"

I thought I was shooting in the dark with that question. I knew for a fact he hadn't been there by the creek that morning. The most logical explanation was that he had gone home after the two Sorensen cousins had passed out in the barn. Villmarkers didn't generally sleep outside of the protection of Villmark.

73

But my heart sank as their faces lit up with surprise.

"Yes, actually," Ralf said. "He woke us up when the others were heading to the creek. He already knew what was going on."

"He heard the others talking about it as they went by," Keith added.

"He said we'd be blamed for sure," Ralf went on. "And in that moment, that felt true."

"You thought my grandmother would blame you for murder?" I asked.

"I don't remember exactly what happened for a good chunk of last night," Keith said. "We might have made it to the bridge at some point. We didn't burn it down, obviously, but we might have left evidence that we were there."

"It seemed smarter to just be gone," Ralf said.

"Does it seem smarter now?" I asked. I must've been channeling my grandmother in that moment, because they both looked down at the toes of their boots and wouldn't meet my eyes.

"No. We should've stayed," Ralf said.

"Okay," I said with a sigh. "Get in your truck and head back to Runde. We're going to be following behind you the whole way."

They both nodded, then turned to climb into their truck. I watched as the truck backed up in a U, then started picking its way along the tree-lined road.

"I don't know what this all means," I said with a sigh.

"Well, I really don't know what this means," Andrew said. "Who's this Roarr person you were asking about?"

"Lisa's fiancé, remember?" I said.

"Oh, yeah, you mentioned him that one time," he said. "Wait, you think the two things are related? But wouldn't the police have already ruled out her fiancé for her murder? I thought they never even had any suspects. Did they know she was engaged?"

"The police knew everything they needed to know," Loke said, steering Andrew by the shoulders towards the passenger side of the car. "We have to get going if we're going to follow them back to Runde."

"Yeah," Andrew said distractedly. I could tell his brain was still whirling.

"Way to go," Loke whispered to me over the roof of the car as he circled the car towards me. I opened my door and pulled the seat forward so he could get in.

"I have questions for you," I whispered back.

"I bet you do," he laughed. "And yet..." He just let his thought trail off as he crawled into the back seat, but I knew what he meant.

I needed to know a ton more about how the protective spells worked, and whether what Roarr was doing was merely mildly worrying or if it was deeply worrying.

Of course it was entirely possible that any conversation with Loke on the topic would be full of his usual maddeningly vague answers and hints that my grandmother knew things she was deliberately keeping from me. Even so, it was a conversation I desperately wanted us to have.

But we couldn't. Not with Andrew in the car.

It was going to be a long, silent ride back to Runde.

CHAPTER 11

*A*s it turned out, a long, silent drive back to Runde would've been pretty nice. But instead I was grilled over and over by Andrew about Roarr. I think in the end I managed to convince him that Roarr had a rock-solid alibi for Lisa's murder, and that no one had ever seriously suspected him in the first place beyond the close connection he had to the victim. If he wasn't convinced, he was at least willing to let it go.

Not that Loke was any help. He had gone back to sleep the moment the Volkswagen's wheels had left the ruts of the overgrown dirt road for the smoother pavement of the Gunflint Trail.

"I guess it's not so weird that I never met this Roarr," Andrew allowed after a long pause in our conversation where he had apparently been mulling it over. "I didn't really see much of Lisa after high school since she went away for college. You said he's from another town."

"Yes, a different town, but I don't remember the name," I said. "You might've seen him at the meeting hall if you'd seen him anywhere. But he's not there a whole lot. I was surprised to see him last night."

"But you said he's not really the troublemaking sort?" Andrew persisted.

"I did say that," I said, biting at my lip. This keeping some truths secret was getting tricky. It was a lot to keep track of and hard to remember it all. "He took Lisa's death hard, though. I hope it was just a momentary lapse."

"Attempted arson?" Andrew asked. "Sounds like a pretty big lapse."

"Well, call it drinking with the Sorensens to the point where arson sounds like fun," I said. "My grandmother knows his parents, actually. I'm sure when I talk to her about this, she'll want to check in and make sure he's doing okay. He'll get the help he needs."

"If you say so," Andrew said doubtfully. Then added, "I guess your grandmother *is* good at that sort of thing."

"She is," I agreed, feeling more inadequate than ever. Magic was only the tip of the iceberg when it came to what I had yet to learn to take up her role as volva. "Not to change the subject, but can you tell me anything at all about Garrett Nelsen? I know you said you didn't know him personally, but just in general, who was he?"

"Well, like I said, he kept to himself," Andrew said. "The fights in school between Sorensens and Nelsens, he was never a part of any of those. He didn't really go in for sports either. He used to hang around the wood shop, but I never saw him make anything. He just liked to admire other people's work. I only mention that because lately he's been selling really cool art to some of the local shops, and I have no idea where he's been getting it from."

"What kind of art?" I asked.

"Wood carvings. Some of them are big, like carved from entire logs, and some are little tchotchkes, but most of the pieces are about a foot or two high." I could see out of the corner of my eye that he was demonstrating the size with his hands, but I didn't look away from the road for more than a quick glance.

"What are they?" I asked.

"Animals, mostly, but also some fantastical things like trolls and dwarves and very dour-looking elves," he said. "I've been seeing them pop up all over just in the last year. I don't know where he's getting them from, but I don't think he's making them himself. Like I said, I never saw him touch a tool in the wood shop in school."

"So he's like a dealer," I said.

"I think so," Andrew said. "There's a shop in Grand Marais that has a lot of his work if you want to stop."

"You mean stop following the Sorensens?" I asked.

"I don't think they're going to run," he said. "It seemed to me that fleeing was something that sounded like a good idea early this morning when, frankly, they were probably still a little drunk from last night. I think they're in their right minds now."

"Yeah, I got that sense too," I said, although I wasn't as willing to chalk it all up to beer.

"We can watch them make the turn towards Runde and then stop off real quick," he said.

"All right. Let's do that," I said.

We reached the highway a moment later and watched as the Sorensens signalled their turn, then headed south towards Runde. But I drove on ahead, following Andrew's directions to a small art store only a block off the lake shore. I parked on the street, and the moment the car engine stopped, Loke sat up in the back seat.

"We're home?" he asked.

"Just making a stop," I said, and got out of the car. I turned to look back at him. "You coming?"

"Yeah," he said, rubbing at his eyes before reaching for the latch to push the seat forward.

The wind had picked up, and the air was moist with lake spray as we stepped out of the car. It was brisk, but not exactly cold. We crossed the street and entered the shop. I hadn't caught sight of the sign, and at first it looked like it sold nothing but cheap tourist crap. But Andrew brushed past the shelves of shot glasses, Christmas ornaments, and other assorted Lake Superior-themed knick-knacks through an open doorway to a second room.

The wares on sale in this room were like night and day with the first. This was real art, and most of it was seriously cool even to my jaded eyes. The shelves were organized by artist, with their name and sometimes a photo or self-portrait of some kind on a plaque. I was distracted by a display of blown glass in abstract shapes that reflected every shade of blue, gray and green that the lake contained. They were like waves frozen in time, but I thought twice about touching them when I saw the price tag.

Yep. This was clearly serious art.

"Ingrid, over here," Andrew said, and I left the glass behind to join him at a series of shelves in the darker back corner of the room. The display was startling; at first glance, I thought the shelves were filled with living animals. Only when they failed to move did I realize they were carved from wood. But they were so lifelike, with expressive eyes and clever poses, I was half-convinced they kept moving whenever I wasn't looking directly at them.

"Those are all carved from local wood," a woman said from behind us. She was an older woman with a chaotic mass of gray curls around her thin face and glasses on a chain perched on her nose. She had just emerged from some back room with a cardboard box in her arms and had stopped before passing us. "Let me know if you have any questions." The name stitched on her smock said Laverne.

"We will," I promised. She smiled, then continued carrying the box to the tourist part of the shop.

"See, the plaque says Garrett Nelsen Woodworking, but there's no photo," Andrew said. This plaque was different from the others, like the artist had carved it himself, the letters that spelled his name jagged like Norse runes. Then I leaned in to get a better look at some sort of swirling pattern after the last letters of the name.

"What's that?" I asked, hovering a finger over the swirl without quite touching it. It looked like a whirlpool, but like the animals it was like every time I looked away it started whirling again.

"I think it's the artist's logo," Andrew said, picking up a little troll figure wearing a hat that looked like a huge mushroom. "Look, it's on all of them." He turned it over and showed me the same pattern carved in the base of the troll figure. I took it from him to get a better look. My fingers got a little charge when they touched the wood. It felt warm, like it was alive, but that was probably just from Andrew's own hands.

"This is nothing like that whistle we saw in the ground," I said. "I couldn't make out the whole logo, but it definitely wasn't this."

"No," he agreed. "But then the whistle was nothing like these pieces either."

"It looked like wood," I said.

"It was, but cheaper stuff," Andrew said. "It was clearly mass produced."

"Maybe just a coincidence that it was there, then," I said. I didn't like the way none of our clues were connected at all. It was maddening.

I didn't realize that Loke hadn't followed us out of the touristy part of the shop until just that moment when he emerged with an amused grin on his face. But that amusement died the moment he saw us, or more specifically, saw the wood pieces behind us.

"Andrew," I said. "Can you ask about the price on that piece? There isn't a tag." I could feel that tag under my fingers but scraped it away with one nail before handing it to him.

"Oh. I thought I saw one before?" he said, turning it over in his hands. "I guess not. I'll go check."

"Thanks," I said, fighting the urge to add that there was no hurry.

The minute he was out of the art room, I turned on Loke. "Tell me."

"This is Villmarker art, and it definitely doesn't belong here," he said.

"Why not?" I asked.

"There are rules about what we give in trade and what we take," he said. "This much stuff, and the quality of the art? You know it's only a matter of time until someone wants to track down the artist."

"They'll think it's Garrett Nelsen," I said, pointing at the name plaque. Loke narrowed his eyes at it.

"I don't think the council will think that's good enough," he said.

"You hate the council," I reminded him.

"I do," he said, and his grin came back. "Did I sound judgy just then? Honestly, I just want to find this artist and shake his hand. He found a way around them. Bravo."

I wasn't sure if he was joking - he sounded genuinely annoyed - but before I could ask anymore questions, Andrew was back. He put the piece back in my hands, naming a price that was very nearly everything I had left in my checking account.

"But the smaller pieces are a little cheaper," he said, gesturing towards an assortment of dwarves in mining poses.

"No, I think it's this one," I said, turning the troll around and around in my hands. I really liked him. His face was totally so-ugly-its-cute, and his high-water pants and tunic with rope belt were incredibly detailed. The mushroom hat was eye-catching, but his boots too looked like some sort of fungal growth.

But I think I had bonded with him when I had touched him. Something had passed into me in that moment. For all I knew, every piece would give me that little charge when I touched it. But that was a really good argument to not keep touching things. I couldn't afford to buy them all.

"I like it too," Andrew said. "Look at his nose. He looks like he's just about to sneeze."

"Fighting a sneeze," I said, looking the troll straight in the face. "My goodness. He must have had some sort of model. A troll-looking person, maybe. It's just so... specific. Individualistic."

"I can show you tons more just like it," Loke whispered close to my ear.

"No, I'm getting this one," I said with finality.

"Why?" he asked. "I don't mean this one. I mean any one."

"Evidence, maybe," I said. He looked like he thought that was a very bad answer. Andrew, again, just looked confused. But I hugged the troll tight. "I'm going to show it to my grandmother. She can help me decide where he goes."

"He's a little big for the mantle," Andrew said as he led the way to the other room, to Laverne and the cash register. "Of course your grandmother does have a massive mantle, so maybe not."

"I'm not joking," Loke whispered to me again. "I can show you tons."

"And you will," I said. "But this one is mine."
"Is this another compulsion?" he asked semiseriously.
"No," I said. "It's just me buying some cool art."
I was almost positive that was true.

CHAPTER 12

$\mathcal{I}$. decided to park my car in the back of the meeting hall parking lot rather than putting it back in Jens Swanson's garage. I had abused his hospitality enough.

Loke and Andrew followed me to my grandmother's house, but when we went inside, we found no sign of her. Her bedroom door was shut, but then it nearly always was. Mjolner was sitting on the rug in front of the cold fireplace, grooming himself. He didn't look up when we came in.

"I think she's still sleeping," I said. "I wanted to show her this piece, but I don't want to wake her."

"No messages," Andrew said, looking at his phone. "I guess that means no one has heard anything from the police yet."

"Well, it's only been a few hours," I said. "Do you have to get to work or anything?"

"Yes, actually," Andrew said. "I have a thing. Unless you needed something else?"

"Just to be sure Keith and Ralf are back," I said. "It's not important. I'm sure they are."

"I'll text Tobias," he said, his thumbs already tapping away.

"Great," I said. "But I don't need you to stay while you wait for an answer. I know how unreliable cell connections can be in Runde. Just let me know when you hear anything, okay? Text me."

"Sure," Andrew said, still typing on his phone. I steered him toward the door as gently as I could. He finished the text to find himself already standing on the front porch. "Oh."

"Thanks for the help this morning," I said brightly. "And if you see your dad, tell him the car is running great."

"Okay, sure," he said. He looked past me at Loke still standing in the kitchen. The look of surprise on his face was morphing to some other thing just as I closed the door.

"Subtle," Loke said.

"We need to get up to Villmark, and we can't do that if he's tagging along," I said.

"Sure," Loke said. "It's just, he probably thinks we're a thing now."

"No, he doesn't," I said. "Who would believe such a thing?"

"Didn't you see the look on his face when you slammed the door? Wounded."

"I didn't slam the door," I said, but I couldn't deny I had been rudely abrupt.

Well, I would happily make it up to him later.

"So, when are you planning on putting that statue down?" Loke asked. I hadn't realized I was still holding the troll cradled in my arms like a baby.

"Oh. I was planning on bringing it up to Villmark with us," I said. "It might come in handy while we look for anything similar."

"I promise you, this isn't going to be a tough search," Loke said. He strolled over to the window and peeked out into the front yard. "He's gone. We can go."

I left my grandmother a note telling her that Keith and Ralf were back - I hoped that was in fact true - and that Loke and I were going up to Villmark. Then I grabbed my walking stick, and we headed out the door.

The sky was still overcast, and the air was getting chilly, especially near the waterfall where we were coated with spray. I was grateful I had thrown on my windbreaker in the rush to leave the house that morning.

I stopped inside the cavern behind the waterfall to wipe the droplets off of the troll with the front of my shirt. "Are you going to call for the Thor?" I asked.

"What do you mean?" Loke asked, then answered his own question. "Oh, that business the others do." He sucked his teeth, a quick tisking sound. "Not necessary."

"But what if the cave is blocked?" I asked, even as I followed him through the cavern to the narrower cave beyond. He grinned at me and made a little wave with his hand. I thought he was joking at first, but then I heard the sound of stone grinding on stone. "Can anyone do that?" I asked.

"No," he said with an even wider grin. "I can teach you. But I'll probably want something in trade."

"I'm good," I said.

The fire in the room beyond was low embers again, barely illuminating the space, but we walked through it without pausing. I wondered who was on guard duty and whether they knew we were there. I was pretty sure they didn't. I didn't think the spell Loke used to move freely between the two towns was just to move stone. He moved back and forth a lot with no one caring.

We emerged in the meadow at the top of the waterfall and continued on for the short walk through the woods before reaching the east end of Villmark. The people were out and about, working and shopping or just standing and chatting. A few who recognized me gave me nods of hello, but people tended to ignore Loke.

"Does it bother you?" I asked.

"Hmm?"

"The way people here pretend not to see you," I said.

"Oh. I hadn't noticed," he said.

I doubted that was true. And yet, I knew very little about him. Not even his family name, or if he had a family, or any real friends in Villmark. Thorbjorn got along with him all right, but Thorbjorn got along with everybody.

"What is your last name, anyway?" I asked.

"It's just over here," Loke pointed, ignoring my question and leading me to the left of the well at the center of town, towards the marketplace.

Well, I could take a hint. "Which shop are we going to?" I asked. I had been to the marketplace before with my grandmother. It was a side street off the main road lined with shops. In all but the worst weather, there were booths as well, selling mainly fresh food.

I could smell freshly baked bread already. Despite the amount of sausage and eggs I had eaten for breakfast, my stomach grumbled.

"It's at the far end," Loke said, and now that I had dropped the personal questions, he slowed his steps to a more leisurely walk. "Lots of people in Villmark carve in wood, but anyone who trades what they make, they trade through Magna's place."

Magna's shop was not exactly on the main road or even right on the marketplace road, I realized as Loke led the way down a half flight of stairs to a basement shop. The marketplace road ran parallel to the slope of the hill, so the back of the basement was probably a walk-out, but this was still the first Villmark basement I had been in. Loke gave the door a little kick, as if he knew it would stick when he tried to open it, and then we were in a darkened space, the low ceiling held up by thick wood rafters every few feet. Very convenient for bumping one's head. I was just short enough not to worry, but Loke had to scrunch up his lanky frame to walk down the sloped aisle between rows of crowded shelves.

"Wow," I said, looking around. "I had no idea there'd be so much." He turned to look at me, raising his eyebrows. "Okay, you said tons. I'm sorry. I thought you were exaggerating."

"As if I would ever stretch the truth," he said, in that tone where it was impossible to decide if he was joking or not.

The shelves were packed close together in rows, but after the last pair of shelves we were in an open space more brightly lit by a wall of windows on the far side. There were two long worktables running across the room, and assorted tools were hanging both from the rafters that were now a respectable height overhead and on the walls to either side.

A middle-aged woman was working at one of the tables, carefully tapping a hammer on the end of a chisel to carve something into the handle of an axe that she held steady in a vise grip. Her long whitish blond hair was braided, but that braid was left to hang down the middle of her back much as my grandmother wore hers. There was a strip of leather worked through the braid like a younger girl might do with a ribbon. She was wearing darker leather pants and a leather apron over a stained white shirt, and her sleeves were rolled up to leave her forearms bare.

Her skin was so darkly brown, and her muscles and bone structure were so strongly defined, she almost looked like she had been carved of wood herself.

She didn't look up when we came in, just continued with her work, only occasionally pausing to blow a curl of wood out of her way. A man stood a step back from the table, and he gave us both a nod of hello, then turned his attention back to the woman.

Loke hopped up on a stool and folded his arms to wait. I turned back towards the shelves to look at what she had on display. There were many tools like axe handles or kitchen spoons or bowls or storage chests. There were also carvings of animals and even trolls like the one I held in my arms. They were all lovely, and clearly very well made.

But none of them felt like they were moving when I wasn't looking at them. None of them felt alive.

"How's that?" the woman said at last. Thanks to Kara and Nilda, I could understand her even though she wasn't speaking English.

"Sure and that's fine," the man said, taking the axe from her and admiring the fresh runes carved into the side. "Here you go," he said, handing her a thick coin. She took it and bounced it on her palm as if checking the weight, then accepted it with a nod. The man left, and she tucked the coin away in a pocket of her leather apron, then turned back to her worktable.

I thought she was going to carry on ignoring us, but then she said, "and what have I done to bring you to my door?"

"We have some questions for you," Loke said, still lounging on the stool. "Magna, this is Ingy."

"Ingrid," I said. No matter how many times I asked, I could never get Loke to stop calling me Ingy. I certainly wasn't going to take it from anyone else. "Ingrid Torfudottir," I clarified.

"I assumed," Magna said, and gestured at the red hair that peeked out from under my cap.

"Ingy is still working on her Norwegian. How's your English?" Loke asked.

"Well enough, I should think. The young folk disagree," she said in English. She spoke slowly, her accent thick but melodic.

"We had some questions for you," I said, speaking a little slower than I usually would to be sure she understood. "What do you know about this?" I crossed the room to set the wooden troll on an open patch of worktable. Magna looked up at it, but her face revealed nothing.

"Are you selling?" she asked, picking up the troll to take a closer look at the carving.

"No," Loke said. "But lots of other people are. Do you recognize it?"

Magna gave him an irritated look, but then turned her attention back to the troll. "I have some like these," she said at last, then pointed to one of the shelves. "Not many. I get them secondhand. What's this mark?" she asked, tapping the logo on the bottom.

"I was hoping you'd know," I said. "I think it's a maker's mark."

"Hm," Magna said, although what that meant I had no clue.

"Magna, we saw dozens of these in a store out in the modern world," Loke said. "Just one store, but I've been told they're in others as well. Far too many."

"You accuse me of something?" she asked, narrowing her eyes at him.

"The council has rules," Loke said.

I didn't know what to make by that. Loke sounded genuinely angry that someone might be breaking the rules. But that would be so... un-Loke.

"I know the council's rules," Magna said. "I sell to no one who does not walk into my shop on their own two feet."

"Has anyone with two feet bought a lot of pieces from you?" Loke asked.

"I do not break the rules," Magna said. "If the council is worried, the council can speak to me directly."

"I think we've gotten off track here," I said. "Loke, we didn't come to accuse anyone of anything. This is a fact-finding mission."

"I do not break the rules," Magna said again. I'm not sure she understood what I had just said.

"Don't you?" Loke asked. He was still sitting on the stool with his arms crossed, but he seemed to be towering over Magna and I. The floor was still sloped here; he was, in fact, higher than we were. But still. I moved closer to him until he just seemed like a normal-sized Loke.

"Loke, we're here about the murder, remember? And there's no way she did that, right?"

"A murder in Runde is one thing," Loke said. "Exposing Villmark to the world is quite another."

"But we don't know that's happening," I said.

"Yet," he said.

"Would you just let me do the talking?" I asked. "If we turn up anything suspicious, you're going to want me to talk to the council anyway, right? Not you?"

He glared back at me, but I knew I had him. Then he started to grin at me, and I knew he knew I knew.

"Carry on," he said with a theatrical sweep of his arm.

I turned back to Magna, who was watching us both with growing annoyance. "I do not break the rules," she said again.

"I know," I assured her. "We... I mean, *I* just wanted to know if you recognized the work. Do you know who made this troll?"

"Of course," she said. "Such work only comes from one pair of hands. But he doesn't sell, ever. He only trades."

"But you said you had some here?" Loke asked.

"He trades with people who sometimes sell," she said.

"Who?" I asked.

"Solvi," Magna said.

"The Solvi who did the carvings on the Viking ship," I said, looking more closely at my troll. The carvings on the ship had been more rudimentary, just decorative touches where the troll was a lovingly rendered complete piece. Still, now that I was looking, I could see the similarities in technique. "Of course."

"Great, thanks for the help," Loke said, hopping off the stool to grab my elbow and propel me out of the shop.

"Thank you, Magna!" I called back over my shoulder. But the minute we were outside, I wrenched my elbow out of his grip. "What is with you today?" I demanded.

"If there's anyone less likely to be moving a lot of Villmark art outside of the bounds of the village and into the modern world than Magna, it's Solvi," he said.

"Really?" I said with as much disdain as I could muster. "Less likely than Magna, you say? After all that just happened down there?"

"Please, I have a reputation to protect," he said with a wave.

"Still, I have to talk to Solvi," I said.

"We're going to need help with that," Loke said.

"Why?" I asked.

"Why?" Loke repeated, and he was grinning at me again. "My dear Ingy, don't you know where Solvi lives?"

"No," I admitted.

"Solvi lives out in the deep, dark woods," Loke said, already leading the way back through the marketplace towards the main road. "And while I'm perfectly happy to traipse through those woods all on my lonesome, you still need a little something more."

"I need a Thor," I said.

"Bingo," Loke said.

CHAPTER 13

I half expected to see Thorbjorn waiting for us at the end of
the northern road when we got there. He always seemed to
know when I needed him. But this time, he wasn't there.

Instead, we found him just inside his garden gate, arming up.

"Looks like we caught you just in time," Loke said. "Patrol?"

"Patrol," Thorbjorn agreed as he buckled a leather bracer to his
arm. Then he looked up at me. "Did you need something?"

"Loke and I were going to talk to Solvi," I said.

"Solvi? What about?" he asked. I held out the troll statue I had been
cradling in my arms and he took it. "Yes, this looks like his work all
right. But why do you need to talk to him about that?"

"We think he has a connection to the murder victim," I said. "The
one under the bridge. He might know something that could help."

"This isn't a matter for your police, then?" Thorbjorn asked.

"I'm not sure yet," I said. "But there's another matter, too. The
murder victim was selling lots of Solvi's work, all up and down the
shore, apparently."

"Solvi is breaking the secrecy rules?" Thorbjorn asked darkly.

"Someone is," Loke said. "Magna says it isn't her, and I believe her."

"No, I don't see her selling to anyone outside our village. That's not her way," Thorbjorn said with a shake of his head. "But Solvi doesn't sell his work at all. He only offers it in trade."

"That's why we have to talk to him," I said. "We need to know who he might have traded with. And if he knew anything about Garrett Nelsen."

"If you're busy, I can take Ingy there myself," Loke said.

Thorbjorn's eyes swept up and down Loke's frame. "You're not even armed."

"Aren't I?" Loke asked as he quirked one eyebrow.

"Clearly, I have to take you," Thorbjorn said, buckling his sword belt around his waist and tucking his axe into its loop on the other side. Then he took up a spear and motioned for us to precede him out of the garden.

We followed the same trail through the meadow that Thorbjorn had taken me down once before, but after reaching the forest he changed directions, heading away from Runde, the highway and the lake and towards the dark mountains on the horizon. The ones that didn't exist in Minnesota.

"Why does Solvi live way out here?" I asked. "Especially if it isn't safe."

"He's perfectly safe," Thorbjorn said. "It's dangerous for you because your magic would attract things."

"My magic," I said, looking down at my perfectly ordinary hands. "I have enough magic to attract trouble, but not enough magic to protect myself?"

"Ironic, right?" Loke said with a laugh.

"Not enough control over your magic to protect yourself," Thorbjorn corrected me. "But that will come."

But as we walked on, deeper into the forest, I became less inclined to talk. It felt wrong, somehow. Like to speak would be to disturb something best left undisturbed. It was so dark, and so silent under the trees.

At first I thought we were walking through shadow because the hill was between us and the sun, but as we walked, I realized that it was nearly midday. The sun would be southerly this time of year, but still more or less above us. Even the clouds overhead weren't thick enough to make it this dark.

No, it was the trees themselves creating the darkness. And yet, they weren't crowded close together like in the woods around the Sorensen hunting cabin. The trunks here were few and widely spaced, and nothing branched off until it was far overhead. Even the evergreens were bare at our level, although the forest floor was thick with many years' worth of their needles.

The sun wasn't the only thing missing here, either. There wasn't so much as a breath of wind. I supposed we were in a sort of bowl between the tall hill overlooking the lake where Villmark stood and the beginnings of the hills still ahead of us somewhere, with more hills close in on either side. But the air felt too still, too quiet. It was like the forest around us was swallowing up any sound we made. Even sweeping my feet through the dried needles and scattered leaves didn't seem to make the correct amount of noise.

Also, it really felt like something was watching us.

"Is something out there?" I whispered to the others. "Something that's watching us?"

"Don't be silly," Loke said with a laugh. But he was whispering too, and his laugh sounded forced.

"It's nothing," Thorbjorn said, but the momentary surge of relief that his words gave me exploded to smithereens when he added, "it's just the trees."

"The trees are watching us?" I asked.

"Well," he drawled, taking entirely too long to end on, "no. It just feels that way because of the way the trees are. In layers, where it feels like you can see through the trunks for miles, but when you try, you realize it's just a few feet."

I looked around and saw that he was right. The layering thing was exactly it. I realized it was like how animators used different cells for the foreground, mid-ground and background, then stacked them up and moved them over each other. Each cell might be sparsely populated with trees, but when they were stacked the gaps between the trees never seemed to line up the way they should.

"How far do we have to go?" I asked, hugging the troll statue close to my chest as if it could warm me.

"Not far," Thorbjorn said, and moved to walk closer by my side. "I didn't think this would bother you so much. We came down here all the time as kids."

"Still don't remember," I mumbled. But I found it incredibly hard to believe I could ever have been unbothered by such a place. Had I at eight been just that brave, or just that foolhardy?

"Here it is," Thorbjorn said a few minutes later, and I looked up to see the path ahead of us opening up into a clearing. The mix of trees became nothing but beech in a ring around that clearing, the branches tangling together as if to form a protective circle. They even still had their autumn leaves of scarlet and gold. Perhaps the lack of wind down here helped those trees hold onto their foliage crowns.

At the center of the clearing stood a little round house with a bright green door, rounded on top but straight down the sides, so not quite like Halldis' round red door that still haunted my dreams. I could see a kitchen garden just on the other side of the house, all dried and brown now but still sporting bean poles arranged like tee-pees at the back of the plot, the desiccated remains of pumpkin vines twined near their bases. There was a woodpile against the other side of the house, another pile of uncut logs a little further away.

But mostly the clearing was full of carvings. A few were former tree trunks that had been carved where they had stood into elaborate dioramas I longed to take a closer look at. Others were freestanding, a variety of animal shapes that had the same quality as the pieces in the store in Grand Marais, like they were moving whenever I looked away. It made it look like the clearing was hosting an animal party, and we three had just interrupted the festivities.

"Solvi!" Thorbjorn called as we stepped into the clearing. We headed towards the door, but stopped as Solvi himself came around the side of the house from the backyard, a hammer and chisel in his hands.

"Thorbjorn," Solvi said. Then his eyes passed to Loke and me. "And guests. I don't often get guests. I'm afraid I have nothing to offer you just now."

"That's all right," I said. "We don't want to intrude. We just had a few questions to ask you."

"Questions," Solvi said, as if he wasn't sure what the word meant. "I'm working on something at the moment, and this time of year the light passes so quickly. Do you mind if you ask your questions while I continue with my work?"

"No, no problem," I said. I'll admit I was a bit disappointed. I was insanely curious to see what was inside his house, especially now that I had gotten a closer look at his door and windows. Everything had subtle decorative touches. It wasn't like a gingerbread house, it didn't have that sort of overwhelming clash of excessively elaborate design elements. It was more like, if two pieces of wood were going to join for functional purposes, he had found the most beautiful way to make that happen. Everything had a flow that suggested water, and I longed to run my fingertips over the patterns in the wood slats of the house walls.

Instead, I followed the others to the back of the house. Besides the kitchen garden which I had glimpsed from the other side, there was also a collection of wood benches around a fire-pit that was currently cold ash but whose blackened, cracked rock borders spoke of many nights of roaring flames and intense heat.

One of those benches had been pulled a little apart from the others and that was where Solvi sat now, returning his attention to an upright log of about half his height which was standing on a low table in front of him. He had just started roughing out a shape, and although there were no details yet, I thought I could make out the outlines of a bear with a fish in its hands.

"First question," Thorbjorn said, and gave me an inquiring look. I nodded that he should go on with what he wanted to ask first. "I don't remember seeing you after the excursion last night."

"Really?" Solvi said. He didn't sound bothered, and his eyes were focused on the sculpture in front of him. He rubbed his thumb over a line that divided the bear's arm from its body but didn't raise his chisel. "I'm not surprised if your memory is faulty, given all the drinking you did. You don't usually even come down to the mead hall. But after such a fine day out on the water, who could resist, eh?"

"Hm, yes," Thorbjorn said, tugging at his beard. "So you were there?"

"Aye," Solvi said, running his thumb over another line carved into the wood and frowning as he made his artistic assessment.

"And someone else who was there could attest to that? Someone with a better memory of last night than me?" he asked, not at all embarrassed to admit to the fault in his own recollection.

"I am, as you know, less inclined to socialize with others than even you," Solvi said.

"I have noticed that, yes," Thorbjorn said. I heard Loke stifle a snicker and shot him a quelling glare.

"But the occasion demanded some form of salute, so I was there in the mead hall with the others, although it's not my natural place." His eyes were still on his work, and he finally chose the place to set his chisel and began tapping away at it with the hammer. "I downed a mug of beer among my fellow travelers, yes, but it was more among them than with them."

"So no one saw you?" Thorbjorn asked.

Solvi kept tapping at his chisel for a moment, not looking up at us or answering. When he finished, he blew the wood dust off the sculpture to assess this new bit of work, and only when he was satisfied with that did he speak. "I saw Roarr, briefly," Solvi said. "But I'll understand that you might not accept his vouching for anyone."

"Roarr is a free man with all legal rights and responsibilities intact," Thorbjorn said. "The council ruled so."

"This is a legal matter?" Solvi asked, finally looking up at Thorbjorn.

"We're still trying to determine that," I said.

Solvi didn't respond, and I wasn't sure if he had even heard me. But then he turned back to the sculpture and raised his chisel and hammer again. "Nora Torfudottir served me my beer."

"Then you were there," Thorbjorn said with an air of finality. "I am sorry I didn't remember seeing you."

"You saw many others," Solvi said diplomatically. "Why does it matter where I was last night?"

"Do you know Garrett Nelsen?" I asked.

"Garrett Nelsen," he repeated, then lapsed into silence as if consulting some mental contacts list.

"This is your work, right?" I asked, thrusting the troll out towards him. He looked up at it with mild surprise.

"Yes, that's mine," he said. "Where did you get it?"

"Is this your mark?" I asked, turning the statue over to show him the spiralling logo on the bottom. He leaned forward on his bench to take a closer look.

"I've never had any need for a mark," he said. "Everyone knows my work. Perhaps someone else added that."

"Garrett, maybe," Loke said to me. But I wasn't so sure. The whirlpool pattern looked like it moved. Not so much on the troll's foot, but definitely on the plaque in the store.

"We should've taken pictures at the art shop," I said back to him, but then turned to Solvi. "Pieces like this are on sale all over the North Shore. Did you know that? I'm certain they are all yours."

"Yes. Garrett Nelsen sells them," Solvi said.

"So you admit to breaking the rules about trade with the outside world," Thorbjorn said.

"No," Solvi said. "No one knows where these come from. We had an agreement."

"Who had an agreement?" I demanded.

Solvi sighed and set his tools down beside him on the bench. "I knew Garrett Nelsen. We met about a year ago, on one of my other infrequent trips to the mead hall. Some of the others had been telling him about my work, and when we met, he asked to see some of it. I agreed. Then we went on from there."

"So you arranged for Garrett Nelsen to take your woodworking out of Villmark and to sell it all over the North Shore?" I asked. "What did you get in return?"

"I? Nothing," Solvi said. "I want nothing. What need do I have for fame or riches? This life I have now, in my little cabin, creating my art with all my waking hours, there is no finer life than this."

"So why involve an outsider like Garrett Nelsen?" Loke asked. "Why not just continue to trade with the other Villmarkers?"

Solvi sighed. "There are only so many of us, and I make so much art," he said, waving his arms to indicate the cluttered clearing around us, fairly stuffed with his art already. "I want nothing for myself, but my art wants to be free. It wants to be seen and appreciated."

"You know Garrett Nelsen is passing all this off as his work, then?" I asked. "The art shop had his name as the creator."

"That is what we agreed," Solvi said. "He says he makes it himself, and that it all comes from Runde. No one ever knows where it is really from."

"But you never got permission from the council," Thorbjorn said.

Solvi waved a hand dismissively. "No need. I wasn't breaking the rules."

Loke laughed appreciatively. "No, as far as I can see, you never were. Technically."

"So you didn't meet him at all last night?" I asked.

"I was on the ship with both of you," Solvi said, taking up his tools and turning his attention back to his sculpture. "Then I was in the mead hall, also with both of you."

"How well do you know Garrett Nelsen?" I asked.

"Not very," he admitted. "We've met only a few times. I leave the pieces in one of his family's barns during the night and he retrieves them later. I believe he tells people that barn is his workshop."

"Do you know any of his other acquaintances? Anyone who would want him dead? Any reason anyone would want him dead?" I asked.

"No," Solvi said. "I know none of his friends. I know nothing of his business in the modern world. For all I knew, he had never sold a single piece of mine. But it is good to know that they are out in the world. Although I suppose now, with Nelsen dead, that's all over."

He looked at the half-formed bear in front of him, and I could very well imagine what he was feeling. It was the worst thing in the world, to feel like your art was never going to be seen by anyone, was never going to matter in a single person's life. In that moment, I could imagine him wondering if it was even worth it, to finish this bear or any other, now that the market hungry for his work had suddenly disappeared.

But then he set the chisel against the wood and raised the hammer once more, and I knew that feeling too. Making art, the process itself, was its own reward.

His clearing was going to get crowded indeed over the months and years to follow, I was sure.

CHAPTER 14

I walked with Loke and Thorbjorn back to Villmark, then continued on alone back to Runde. My head was in a whirl, but it was a whirl of dead ends.

I believed Ralf and Keith Sorensen when they said they only planned to torch the bridge and hadn't even stayed awake long enough to get that done.

I believed Solvi that he had only wanted to share his art with the world, even if it was a world that he himself would never walk in. What a strange and lonely feeling that must be.

My fondest wish for years was to see my art in a book in a bookstore, to see people take it down and page through it and show the illustrations to each other. I couldn't imagine never knowing if what I did ever brought anyone any joy. But Solvi, spending his days apart from even his quiet community, clearly felt differently.

A lot of people seemed to know who Garrett Nelsen was, and yet no one seemed to have known him well. I knew the police would be interviewing his family, and if they uncovered any close friends, they would be interviewing them as well. Perhaps this really was just a Runde matter. Worse, perhaps it had just been a random thing, and there would be no solving it.

I didn't like that thought at all.

It was nearly one in the afternoon when I came up the front steps and opened the door into my grandmother's cabin. I was half expecting her to still be sleeping, but she was up, sitting at the kitchen table with a cup of coffee in front of her. She was dressed, but when she looked up, I suspected I had just startled her out of another doze.

"Ingrid," she said. "What do you have there?"

"Something that Solvi carved," I said, setting the troll down on the table in front of her. "I bought it in Grand Marais."

"Grand Marais," my grandmother said as she examined the piece. "You've just come from Villmark. Does the council know?"

"You can tell I was just in Villmark?" I asked.

"The magic between the worlds leaves a trace on people who cross over," she told me. "You'll be able to see it yourself soon enough. The council?"

"From what I gather, they didn't know before, but Thorbjorn is probably telling them now," I said. "It doesn't really matter, since nothing else will be leaving the village now. Solvi was bringing it out of Villmark to one of the Nelsen barns in Runde, and Garrett Nelsen was selling it as his own art. But now that Garrett is dead, that trade route died with him."

"This mark is Solvi's mark?" my grandmother asked, frowning at the spiral on the bottom of the troll's boot.

"He says no, but I don't think I believe him. Why? Does it mean anything?" I asked.

"No, it's just clearly not a Villmark thing," she said. "Solvi, if he signed his pieces, would likely use a rune sigil. This is very swirly."

"There was one in the store on a plaque that looked like it was actually moving. I think it's meant to invoke the lake or the weather or something," I said.

"Maybe both," my grandmother agreed, then set the troll back down to take another sip at her coffee.

"I don't know anything more about the murder than I did this morning," I said. "The two Sorensens had been planning some mischief with the new bridge, and were afraid that if you asked them about the murder you would just know about the bridge thing, which is why they ran."

"You do know I can't actually read minds?" she said to me.

"Oh, sure," I said, although I was far from sure about any such thing. "But you do have a way of making a person want to confess anything they're guilty of."

"It's in the stare," she said, pointing at her own eyes as she narrowed them suspiciously. "You'll learn it."

"That could come in handy," I said. "So anyway, Andrew told me that Garrett sold these pieces to art stores all over the shore, so I went to see one of the stores in case it was important. It was clearly Villmark stuff, so Loke and I went to Magna's shop, and she sent us on to Solvi. But Solvi has a solid alibi and, honestly, doesn't seem like the murdering type. So that was another dead end."

"There's no such thing as a murdering type," my grandmother said. "Anyone can be pushed to that extreme, given the right circumstances. Or rather, the wrong ones."

"Well, he was in the meeting hall with the rest of us after the ship docked, so that rules him out."

"Yes, I remember seeing him," my grandmother said. "He left with some of the other Villmarker men. They looked like they were going to continue the party back in the village since it was only just past midnight. But I absolutely couldn't keep the spells up any longer in the meeting hall."

"Are you opening again tonight?" I asked.

"Sure, but after last night, I'm sure it will be a smaller crowd," she said with a reassuring smile. But the dark circles under her eyes were anything but reassuring.

"I wish I could help you. I feel so useless," I said.

"Well, it sounds to me like you've already done exactly what I asked you to," she said. "You've searched every avenue of inquiry that led back to Villmark and ruled them all out. What happened to Garrett Nelsen was tragic, especially so soon after the loss of Lisa. And knowing those two families, there will be repercussions I'll have to deal with. So many emotions to sort out. But the murder itself, I think we can safely declare a police matter. It's out of our hands."

"Yeah, maybe," I said.

"You don't sound convinced," she said.

"I just want to check a few more things to be sure," I said. "Starting with this swirly thing." I tipped the troll over to rest him on his back, then took a picture of the logo with my phone. I started to run a search on the image, but my grandmother's crappy wifi locked up right away, and I had just one bar down in the river valley.

"Heading up to Jessica's?" my grandmother guessed.

"Yeah," I said. "I have to check my email and stuff, anyway. It's just easier to do it there. Do you need anything from up on the road?"

"No, I'm just about to head over to the meeting hall, anyway. Tuukka is bringing in another batch of honey this afternoon."

"Okay," I said. "I'll catch up with you there."

I left the troll there lying on his back as if he were dozing away the afternoon on our kitchen table, then headed back outside. The sky was still overcast, but it wasn't getting any darker, and at least there was no hint of rain. Today could be as cloudy as it liked; yesterday had been gorgeous, and that was when it had mattered.

I climbed the steep path up the bluff to once more emerge behind the gas station, then crossed the highway to the newest of the collection of buildings gathered around the crossroads: Jessica's bookstore café. For the locals, it also doubled as an internet café, since everyone's wifi down in the valley was as slow and spotty as my grandmother's, and the cell service was even worse.

The bell over the door chimed as I pushed my way inside, and Jessica emerged from behind the counter of assorted pastries. Her coveralls and the blonde braids that formed a crown around her head were both dusted with flour.

"Hey, Ingrid!" she said. "I thought you were coming today."

"Did I say I would?" I asked. I didn't remember any such conversation, but it would be totally like me to forget something like that.

"No, but Mjolner showed up about ten minutes ago and made

himself at home on the footstool by your favorite computer. I figured he knew something I didn't," she said.

"Sounds like he knew something *I* didn't," I said. "But I do need to use the computer. If that's okay?"

"Well, as you can see, it's pretty busy here today," she said, sweeping her hands to encompass the empty bookstore and café nook around her. "Take all the time you need."

"I've narrowed down which illustrations I'm going to frame for your wall," I said as I settled into the chair in front of the computer. "I just have to get the frames."

"No hurry," Jessica said with a wave of her hand. "This is the slow time of year, you know. It'll pick up again next month when the ski slopes open, though. I'll have my espresso machine by then. You'll definitely want to have your art up when the tourists get here."

"Sure," I said, typing in my password to check my email. Nothing but junk. Still no response from anyone I had sent my art out to.

"Say, Jessica?" I said as I logged out of my email and opened a search page. "I'm checking this online, but maybe you already know what it is. Have you ever seen this mark before?" I showed her the picture on my phone. She took the phone from me and used her fingers to zoom in and examine the image more closely.

"No, I don't think so," she said. "What is it?"

"I think it's an artist's logo," I said. "Andrew and I were in Grand Marais this morning and I bought this cute little troll. Well, not exactly little. He's over a foot tall. I probably should've taken a picture of that too. Well, I can show you later. But it has this mark on its foot and I was curious what it meant."

"You and Andrew went to Grand Marais," Jessica said, raising her eyebrows questioningly.

"We were doing an errand for my grandmother," I said. "The art shop side trip was just because it was on the way home."

"A-ha. Sure," Jessica said.

"Do you have a cable..." I trailed off, vaguely gesturing between my phone and the computer.

"Check that drawer," Jessica said, heading back behind her counter.

I opened the desk drawer to my left and found a tangled jumble of cords. With a little work, I found one that connected my phone to the computer so I could transfer the photo. I had just hit go on the image search when the bell over the door chimed.

"Hey, you were right, she is here," Michelle said as she came in with three plates wrapped in foil stacked in her hands. She had pulled a jean jacket on over her waitress uniform, and her honey blonde hair was in a neat ponytail, so I knew she had come over from the middle of her shift at the restaurant on the other side of the highway. "Hey, Ingrid."

"Hi, Michelle," I said. "Is one of those for me?"

"Fish and chips," she said, handing me one of the plates.

"My favorite," I said, my stomach rumbling at the words "fish and chips" and then more loudly when I peeled back the foil and got a whiff of the breaded and fried whitefish, fresh from the lake I could just see over the treetops out the window between two bookshelves. "Thanks! I didn't even realize I was hungry."

"Mjolner was pretty insistent," Jessica said as she came back out from behind the counter with a tray of tea things.

"Mjolner told you I was hungry?" I asked. I had often suspected he could talk and only chose not to, but I admit I was a little hurt that he would choose to talk to others first.

"Well, Michelle and I were on the phone talking about lunch, and he just kept meowing and giving me this look, you know?" Jessica said as she poured out the tea. Michelle unwrapped a turkey club sandwich and set it in front of Jessica, who gave her a nod of thanks.

"I know that look," I said. "Although frankly, he might've been signaling the fish and chips because that's his favorite as well."

Mjolner was still curled up on the overly padded footstool, but he lifted his head with a meow and fixed me with his yellowish-green eyes until I held out a bit of fish for him on the end of my finger. He took it from me with a delicate bite, then licked the juice from my fingertip.

"So what are you working on?" Michelle asked as she unwrapped her own plate of scrambled eggs with salsa that, I knew from experience, was far too picante for my tastes even without the slices of jalapeño that were too excessive to be a mere garnish. She took a huge bite, then pointed at my computer screen with her fork. "What is it?" she asked through a mouthful of eggs.

"It's some kind of logo," I said. I scrolled through the results, but they all seemed to be connected to websites for various stores up and down the coast. The kind that sold local art. "Do you recognize it?"

"Nope," Michelle said. "Jess?"

"No, but I'm not really an art person," she said. Then her cheeks flushed as if she had just put her foot in her mouth. "But I'm definitely going to be learning all about it, now that I've designated a few walls for galleries of local artists."

"I didn't recognize it either," I said. "I think it belongs to Garrett Nelsen."

"Garrett Nelsen that was murdered last night?" Michelle asked.

"So the news has spread," I said.

"Did you know about Garrett before or after you bought that troll thing?" Jessica asked.

"Before," I admitted.

"Are you thinking his work will go up in value now that he's dead?" Michelle asked.

"No!" I said. "I mean, it might, but that's not why I bought that troll. I just wanted to show it to my grandmother. We're trying to figure out who Garrett is as a person, maybe understand what happened."

"I never really knew him," Jessica said as she picked apart her sandwich, just eating the bacon. "I mean, I knew who he was. Everyone knew who the Sorensens and the Nelsens were in high school, you know? But he was older, so our paths didn't cross."

"I didn't know him either," Michelle said. "But the police are working on it, right?"

"Oh, sure," Jessica said with a humorless laugh. "The same police that have never solved Lisa's murder. Let's trust them with this one, too."

I bit my lip. As much as I had wondered how Lisa's parents were holding up, it was all too clear that Jessica was still hurting and angry.

And there was nothing I could say to make her feel better.

I looked down at the food still waiting on my plate, but I had no appetite now. Mjolner opened one eye, watching my plate for the moment I left it unattended. I turned to set it on the far side of the computer monitor where he couldn't reach it.

Or, at least, not easily.

"Jess, I know you're still upset," Michelle said, reaching across the table to clutch her friend's trembling hand. "I understand, really I do. Sometimes the truth never gets exposed. It sucks, but it's just true. We just have to trust that larger forces are still at play. That the universe has its own ways, and that the arc of time bends towards justice. Right?"

I looked from Michelle to Jessica, not sure how she would take this. Would she laugh, throw Michelle's words back in her face? Her anger was still there, in the way she scrunched her eyes shut to keep the tears from spilling and dug her nails into her own palms.

But when she opened her eyes, she was visibly calmer. "You're right," she said. "That's all we have left, to trust in mysterious forces."

"I know it sounds empty, but really, what other choice is there?" Michelle asked.

"None," Jessica agreed, nodding as she gathered up the remains of our lunch. "No other choice at all."

I looked at Michelle, trying to gauge how much she had meant what she just said. Michelle looked back at me, then tipped her head to indicate Jessica, who had her back to us now as she crossed the room to throw the trash away in the bin. We were both thinking the same thing.

The only other choice was nursing the hurt and betrayal of the universe, of turning more and more bitter by the day. And both of us would do anything to steer Jessica away from that if we could.

I hoped Michelle's words helped. It was certainly more than I could manage.

CHAPTER 15

*M*ichelle and I left the bookstore café together, although Mjolner elected to stay behind with Jessica. Well, my grandmother had told her that every bookstore needs a resident cat. Perhaps Mjolner would take that position.

"Going back to work?" I asked Michelle as we waited for the traffic to pass so we could cross the highway.

"Yeah, for a few more hours," she said. "What about you?"

I shrugged. "I was hoping to learn more about Garrett Nelsen, but even with that spelling there are just too many of them in Minnesota. I can't chase all those hits."

"And if you narrow it down to Runde, zero hits," Michelle guessed, which, as a matter fact, was exactly what had happened when I had tried it. "If you want to wait a minute, I can ask my mom."

"Your mom?"

"Yeah," Michelle said, then tugged at my sleeve. We both ran across the highway and stopped at the gas station. We were crossing at a crosswalk, and people knew to look for those around the bridges because there were so many scenic overlooks and parks on the north shore, but you never knew for sure that any given driver saw you.

Michelle turned to me. "I never knew Garrett, but I think my mom knew his mom. She's in the office now doing some paperwork, but if you want to wait, I'll go in and see if she knows where he lived. It'll save you going door to door. The half of that side of Runde that isn't a Sorensen is a Nelsen, you know."

"Yes, that I did know," I said with a sigh. "Thanks!"

I watched as Michelle ran inside the restaurant, greeted the man working in the kitchen, then jogged across the dining area to the back room.

It was a shame my grandmother was too busy to go with me on my little mission, but I knew once she settled in at the meeting hall, she wasn't inclined to leave it again. I think it was easier for her to feed the spells throughout the day rather than try to summon up the power all at once in the evening. At least, that's what I seemed to feel going on when I was there with her. Still, talking to the murder victim's parents felt like something she was better able to do than me. What could I even say?

"Hey," Michelle said as she came back outside. She had a slip of paper in my hand and thrust it at me. "The streets have names, but you'd never know it to try driving around down there, so she drew you a map. I have to get back to work. You got this?"

"I got this," I said, glancing over the map. She had drawn in the bridge, and I swear she had drawn it all shiny. Did everyone know it was steel now? "Tell your mom thanks."

"Sure thing," Michelle said, then disappeared back in the restaurant.

I crossed the highway then followed the path down to the river valley, initially in the direction I had taken that morning towards the bridge, but then across a fallow field further up the gorge towards the waterfall.

Well, that location certainly made it easier for Solvi to sneak things into the barn.

The scattered farmhouses looked alike, but Michelle's mother's map was quite specific on the details, both the house I was looking for and all the houses I was not. I passed by the house with white trim and yellow shutters, then the house with yellow trim and yellow shutters, until I saw the house with yellow trim and white shutters. None of these places had seen a fresh coat of paint in years, and the siding was all the same shade of beige, but I was certain I had found the right place.

The road it was on ended abruptly just beyond its yard with no turnaround or anything, just a row of concrete blocks designed to stop a car from colliding with the rock bluff just a few inches beyond them. I walked up the driveway, climbed the stairs to the creaky porch and knocked on the door.

By the fourth time I knocked, I was pretty sure they weren't home. Maybe they were still at the police station, or had gone to be with family. I looked in the windows, but there was definitely no one inside.

I was about to just leave, when on impulse I walked around the house to the backyard. A clothes line hung limp and empty, running between the kitchen door and the back corner of the garage. Behind the garage was nothing but farm fields, empty this late in the year save for a few broken cornstalks. But at the edge of that field was a barn, and a surprisingly modern one at that. The house and garage were both faded and old and had the look like the winter wind would blow right through them.

But that barn looked snug and warm.

I looked behind me at the road, but there was no sign of any traffic, so I crossed the yard to check out that barn.

I knew I was on to something when I saw the police tape. Solvi had said Garrett told people the barn was his workshop, where he made the pieces he told everyone were his. This had to be the place. Had the police found any evidence? Was I likely to find anything now, after they'd already gone over it?

I ducked under the tape that barred the bottom of a staircase that ran up the side of the barn to another door on the second level. I would've thought this would be for hay storage. The toy farm I had as a kid came with plastic hay bales to put up there and a pulley system to move them from the open door on the second level to the back of the plastic farm truck (sold separately). But when I turned the handle of the unlocked door and stepped inside, I found myself in a nice little apartment. It looked like the sort of place that people usually built over garages, just big enough for a single person in their early twenties who wanted a little independence from their folks but couldn't quite afford to get a place of their own.

I guessed that was Garrett. But I had gotten the sense that Solvi's art had been selling well. So what had he done with all that money? I knew he hadn't been giving it to Solvi, who had no use for it. Or had he built the barn with the money?

The little kitchenette was messy, but didn't seem particularly revealing. Beyond it was a little nook built into the wall with a drop-down desk and a folding chair set in front of it. I could see a rectangle clearly defined in the dust there. The police had taken his computer, then. The drawers of a filing cabinet set next to it were similarly left just a little bit open, enough for me to see they were quite empty. Well, what had I expected?

And yet, I wasn't really here to find clues to the murder. No, what I had a nagging need to find was some sense of who Garrett had been. I had never met him at the meeting hall or around Runde; I was sure of that. And no one else seemed to have any sense of who he was, not even Solvi.

But the things the police had left behind told me little. He had books on a shelf under a window, but they looked like he had bought them all at a secondhand shop and just piled them in there. The topics had no relation to each other, and some were exceedingly dry. Was he really kicking back in the evening with farm reports from the 1950s?

I continued on around the room to his bed. The police had torn it apart, leaving the mattress a little askew on the frame, and on impulse I pushed it back into place with a knee. Then my foot nudged something under the bed. I dropped down on my hands and knees and pulled out a cardboard box. The top flaps had been opened and then folded back down to fit under the bed. The moment I pulled it out, they sprang open again.

It was full of whistles, neatly stacked to fill the entire space. A slip of paper I guessed was an invoice was tucked down one side.

They were exactly like the whistle Andrew and I had found at the shore of the creek. I could see that what we'd been looking at that was printed on the side was a logo, an M and an N side by side. Did that mean anything? I had no clue. I took one and stuffed it in my pocket, then kicked the box back where I had found it.

I couldn't imagine a place that felt less related to magic or Villmark or any of that, and yet, as my grandmother always said, I had to be sure. But how?

I looked around, then chose one of the stools pulled up to the counter in the kitchenette. I sat down and quieted my thoughts, a process that had gotten easier in the last month. At least I was making progress on something, right?

Once I was in my calmest state, I tried looking around again. But nothing jumped out at me. Nothing was begging for my attention or showing me a pattern that hid a secret meaning or anything.

I needed a more active sort of magic, something I could ask questions of, not just wait for answers that always required me to reverse engineer what the question might have been before I could properly understand it. But I hadn't learned any.

I half-closed my eyes and opened my senses the way my grandmother had been teaching me, but whenever I tried to direct those senses around me, my concentration kept just falling apart. I tried a few times, but I kept breaking down faster each time.

Back in the diner I had worked at in St. Paul from sixteen until the day I moved to Runde, during slow times my friend Jesús who worked in the kitchen used to show me how he could wiggle his ears, either one alone or both at once, how he could twitch his nose or flare his nostrils, how he could make his eyebrows do practically anything at will. He had tried to teach me, but it was like those muscles just didn't answer signals coming from my brain. I could just barely make my nose move like a rabbit, but nothing more.

This felt like that. Like I should be able to control these things, but that like my facial muscles, the magic just wasn't answering signals that came from my brain.

I was a bit of a failure as a witchy investigator.

I put the stool back where I had found it, then went back outside, pulling the door closed behind me. I went down the steps and ducked under the police tape, then crossed the yard to get back out onto the road.

The wind picked up, holding a bit of the cold from the lake that I couldn't quite see from this far inland. I wished I had my hat, or at least my gloves. Instead, I shoved my hands into the pockets of my windbreaker.

And felt the whistle I had taken on a whim from the box under the bed. This whistle wasn't a clue, but the one by the creek might be one. Had the police taken it?

I turned my steps, heading not towards home but back towards the murder scene.

CHAPTER 16

I stood rather stupidly for far too long on the shore of the creek under the bridge, looking at the little numbered flag that marked the spot where the whistle had been just that morning.

I don't know what I thought would be different. Clearly it was evidence. Andrew surely would have pointed it out to the police. So why had I been compelled to come here?

I pressed a hand to my forehead. Perhaps that little bit of magic I had done the day before with the waterfall had drained me more than I had realized. I had gotten up a bit earlier than usual, but I had gone to bed way earlier than usual. I had gotten a full night's sleep and then some. I shouldn't be feeling this tired or this disoriented.

It must've been the spell or whatever I had done with the waterfall. That was the only thing that made sense. And yet, in that moment, it hadn't felt like I was doing anything besides sketching a thing I wanted to see.

The problem with my magic was that I couldn't direct it. It preferred to lead me around. Only I never knew if I was being led around by it, or my own whimsy, or by some external force.

I shivered at the thought. The memory of being completely in

Halldis' power was never far from my mind. No matter how I tried to push it away, it always came back.

I headed back up to the highway, my hand in my pocket rubbing at the stamp on the side of the whistle. It hadn't been carved; I knew that. Like Andrew had said, they were mass produced. It had been stamped by a machine. Still, someone had drawn the logo once, before it became a machine stamp. It must mean something to someone.

I took it out of my pocket and looked at it again. It was nothing like a rune, and given the angular letters it would've been very easy to make it look runic. But it was also nothing like the swirling pattern on Solvi's woodworking pieces. The letters were drawn quite boxy, as if to suggest skyscrapers, the diagonal lines becoming like shadows. Was this a Garrett original design? Or had he paid someone to create this logo for him? There were tons of websites that hooked any business owner up with a designer to do just that. Maybe this pattern really did mean nothing.

I put it back in my pocket and trudged on across the bridge. I wanted my sketchpad. Maybe drawing would trigger something in my brain.

I should probably find Thorbjorn first, though. Every time I had successfully used magic, he had been there. Maybe he was like my lucky charm.

Yes, home to get my art bag, and then up to Villmark to find Thorbjorn.

Who was on patrol. Ugh.

My imagination conjured up the image of the plan I had just formed in my mind like a delicate arrangement of sticks suddenly going up in smoke. But at least it was artful smoke, all delicate tendrils and long, looping lines.

I must've gone deeper into my imagination than I had thought, because when I looked up I found myself standing inside the garage behind the gas station again. I was standing at the end of the stall where my car had been until that very morning. Why had I walked there?

"Ingrid?" Jens asked, poking his head around the open hood of a truck.

"Andrew?" I asked.

Apparently, I was there to see Andrew.

"Upstairs," he said, pointing up with one thumb before disappearing behind the truck hood again.

I looked around and saw no sign of any stairs, but there was a ladder against one wall that ran up to a hatch in the ceiling. I climbed up it, hooking an arm through the top rung so that I could use the other to push open the hatch. It wasn't heavy, and it fell open with a clang.

"Sorry!" I called. Then Andrew's face appeared over me.

"Ingrid," he said, sounding surprised to see me. "Do you need help?"

"No, I can do it," I said, pulling myself up onto the floor of the loft. I wasn't sure if that floor was even nailed down or anything; it appeared to be just wide planks of wood set across the steel girders like rafters. "What is this place?" I asked as I looked around.

"Normally, it's just storage," Andrew said as he took a few steps backwards to give me more room. "But my dad doesn't really use it much, so I've taken it over."

Behind him was a boat, or at least the beginnings of a boat. It had to be 25 feet long, resting on six sawhorses that were shaped to hug the curve of the boat's hull.

"I thought your workshop was down by the lake," I said as I got up from the floor, careful of the variety of tools that hung from the low ceiling. Most of them looked quite sharp.

"It is," he said. "It's not big enough for this baby, though."

"What kind of boat is it?" I asked, reaching out to touch the wood of one of its ribs. It felt new: newly cut, newly sanded, almost still a tree.

"It's a canot du nord," Andrew said with a proper French accent. "North canoe. It's for a charity auction that's going to be in Duluth next month. It's not just my work, though. There's a whole team of us, just some folks that are into the history of the voyageurs and like to work with our hands. This is our fourth canot du nord. They're fun to make, but kind of a pain to keep since they're so big. And this is the smaller type. The canot de maître were even longer."

"I had no idea you made boats," I said. "I thought you made furniture."

"That too," he said. "Here, feel the weight of this oar." He handed me a wooden oar with a big grin on his face. I braced myself since it looked sizable, and I didn't know of any way to hollow out wood, but what he handed me was lighter than plastic. "White cedar. See why they used it?"

"Sure, light for portage," I said, handing the oar back to him. "This is beautiful."

"It's not even done yet," he said. "I was just going over the frame one last time. When the guys get off work, we're going to start the birch bark part of the boat." Then he gave me a sidelong look. "But I'm guessing that's not why you're here."

"No, I wanted to show you something," I said, digging in my pocket for the whistle.

"This isn't from the creek?" he asked me as he took it.

"No, this is another one. But it's the same, right? We couldn't see the logo before, but now we can. Do you recognize it?"

Andrew turned the whistle over and over in his hands, but in the end just shook his head. "No. MN, like for Minnesota, maybe? No idea. Where did you find this?"

"It belonged to Garrett," I said. "He had a whole box of them. But I don't know why."

"Well, it does look like swag," he said. "You know, something you give to people so they remember your company. Like at a trade show or something."

"Maybe I should go back to the shop in Grand Marais, see if the store owner recognizes it," I said. "Maybe Garrett gives them to people when he sells them his art. Although, why doesn't it have the swirling pattern logo on it?"

"Yeah, this doesn't look like an update of the other design at all," Andrew agreed. "I suppose there's only one way to find out."

"Drive back up there," I said.

"You don't sound very enthused," he said, handing me back the whistle.

"It's probably just going to be another chase after another dead end," I said.

"Well, I mean, the police are working on it," Andrew said. He was looking over at me from time to time, but his attention was mainly back on the boat and whatever he was checking over. He wanted to be done before his friends came. I got it.

"I know," I said with a sigh.

"Your grandmother worries," Andrew said, speaking a little bit louder since there was an entire boat between us now. "Everyone in Runde has been like her adopted family for as long as I can remember. I guess that didn't really change just because you, her actual family, came back into town."

"She feels responsible," I said.

"It seems like you feel responsible too," he said. "And to think when you came here, you acted like you didn't even think you'd be staying."

"I did not," I said, then tried to remember back to our first conversations together. "Did I?"

"You did," he said. "But that changed in a hurry. Perhaps we grew on you."

"I guess I do feel responsible, but only because my grandmother has been alone for so long. I don't know why she does everything she does. I just know I want to help as much as I can. Is that weird?"

"Not at all," Andrew said. He came back around the far side of the boat and walked up to me, hands in the pockets of his jeans. There was sawdust caught in the knot-work of his sweater again. I guess I knew from where this time.

"I want to check on all this so I can tell her that she didn't miss anything," I said, looking down at the whistle in my hand. "I don't want her to think even for a second there was something she should've sensed, something she should've known about. Some way she could've saved Garrett from his fate. But I need to know more about what happened before I can assure her of that."

"Sure," Andrew said, taking the whistle from me again to give it a second examination. "Yep. We definitely need to go back to Grand Marais. We have a few hours before the shop closes. Shall we?"

"You're coming with?" I asked.

"Well, there is nothing to do here but wait until the others get off work," he said, pulling out his phone to check the time. "Plenty of time to get to Grand Marais and back."

"Okay, great," I said. "Do you want me to pull the car around?"

"I can walk to it with you," he said. Then he leaned past me to turn off the work lights over the ship.

Typically, white cedar has a milder scent than the dark red varieties, but in that moment, I found it pretty overwhelming. I felt myself sway towards it, to breathe it in more deeply.

Which totally looked like I was trying to smell Andrew. I pulled myself back upright with the snap of a military recruit.

"You okay?" Andrew asked. His face was light and shadow in stark relief thanks to the strong but indirect light coming up through the hatch from the garage below.

"Fine!" I said, too quickly maybe, and all but lunged through the hatch to climb down the ladder where the smell of engine oil and gasoline could clear my head.

I would be leaving that last bit out of any summary of my investigation that I gave my grandmother.

Not that it would matter, I thought with a sigh. She'd know anyway. And I would know she knew from that little smile that just barely curled the corner of her mouth. Maybe she could read minds.

CHAPTER 17

*L*averne in the art shop was initially happy to see us. Perhaps she thought she'd get a second sale of one of her expensive high-end pieces, a rarity outside of the tourist season.

But her wide smile melted away when I handed her the whistle.

"Do you recognize it?" I asked.

"Yes," she thrust it back at me. "I had hoped I had talked him out of it, but I guess not."

"Talked who out of what?" I asked.

"Garrett Nelsen, the artist whose piece you bought this morning?" she said, giving me a suspicious look that I didn't know what she was referencing already.

"Of course," I said. "But this logo isn't like what's on the other pieces?"

"No," she said with a sigh. "He decided to rebrand everything before he opens his store. That's the what I was trying to talk him out of. His work sells really well, but I won't be able to get any more of it once I sell what I have left in stock. Which is a shame. I loved his work. I hand-sold a lot of pieces for him, especially in the early days. But I guess loyalty is dead, right?"

Andrew and I exchanged a look. Was this a lead?

"Garret Nelsen was opening a store?" I asked.

"*Is* opening a store," she corrected me. "It's just a block over and half a block up. They plan to be open before the winter tourist season starts."

"I'm sorry," I said. "I thought you knew. Garrett Nelsen died this morning."

"Oh, no!" she gasped, covering her mouth with her hand. As annoyed as she had seemed with him just a moment before, her distress at the news felt genuine. "But how?"

"Murder," Andrew said. "But if the police have any suspects, they haven't told the family yet."

"You know his family?" she asked.

"A little," Andrew said. "We're from the same hometown."

"Oh, yes," she said, nodding. "That little town near here. The name always escapes me. Isn't that funny? There are only so many towns on the North Shore."

"People tend to forget Runde," Andrew said. "It's tucked out of sight from the highway."

"Did Garrett upset a lot of people when he stopped selling his art through their stores?" I asked.

"Oh, I suppose I wasn't the only one to be a bit annoyed, but even as popular as he was, there wasn't enough money involved to lead to *murder*, surely?"

"Will it go up in value, now that he's gone?" Andrew said.

"Not really," she said. "He hadn't made enough of a name for himself just yet. In a few years, maybe that might've been a thing. But now, I'm afraid by next summer no one will even remember him. Which is a shame. He had a real gift."

"You said he was rebranding his art to sell through his own store-front," I said, holding up the whistle again.

"Yes," she said with a sigh. "I've been waiting for the store to open to see what he's offering. If he's drastically changed his style, having older pieces with a different mark in my shop, I might have to adjust my pricing. Depending on whether it was a big change or a small one, and of course the quality of the work itself."

"And he was doing all this himself? Getting the store up and running on top of creating?" I asked.

"Oh, goodness, no," she said. "He had a partner. A local young man named Kyle Meeks. Kyle's parents run a pretty successful café right off the highway, but I gather he was hoping not to follow them into the restaurant business."

"Kyle Meeks," I repeated. Meeks and Nelsen. That's what the MN meant. "Well, we've taken up enough of your time. Thanks for the help."

"Help with what?" she asked. "You're not cops?"

"No, just helping out the family," Andrew said.

"Well, tell them from me that I'm sorry for their loss," she said. "I think I'll move his work up to the front of the store. Make a nice display, like a memorial."

"That sounds lovely," Andrew said. "I'll pass on your thoughts. Thank you."

We headed back out onto the street and were met by a gust of cold air blowing in off the lake. I looked up at the sky, but it was still only overcast. No storms were brewing.

"Should we find that shop?" Andrew asked.

"Definitely," I said. Her directions had sounded vague to me, but Andrew just set off walking like he knew exactly where he was going, and I hurried my steps to keep up with him.

"It doesn't make a lot of sense, killing Garrett because he was no longer going to be selling art through the stores," I said. "Consider what I paid for that troll, and that was a mid-sized piece. Maybe selling one or two a day of those? I'm just guessing at the math, but it doesn't seem like enough money to murder someone over."

"No. And it felt more personal, didn't it?" Andrew asked.

"What do you mean?" I asked.

"Well, like Luke said, that fishing spear wouldn't have done it," he said. "Whoever stabbed him must have held him underwater until he stopped fighting. That's a long time to sustain a murderous impulse."

"If that's what happened," I said. "The stabbing could have been intentional but the drowning accidental."

"They'll probably know more after the autopsy, I suppose," Andrew said. "Look, this is it."

I looked at the shop window he was pointing at. The MN logo was painted on the glass. It looked very new. But there was a closed sign in the corner, and the door was locked when Andrew tried it. He knocked loudly.

I pressed my face to the glass, shading my eyes with my hands to peer inside the unlit space within, as Andrew knocked a second time. After the third time, when the knocking was more like pounding, I saw a man emerging from the back room. Despite being in a shop in the middle of the afternoon, he looked like we had just gotten him out of bed. He was in stockinged feet, and the elaborate shape of his bedhead was epic.

He opened the door, but only wide enough to spit, "we're closed" out at us.

"Kyle Meeks? We need to talk to you," I said.

"Well, I don't need to talk to you," he snapped back at me. "We're not open for business. We're never going to be open for business. So just go away."

He tried to shut the door, but Andrew thrust his toe into the gap just in time. I saw him wince as his foot was ground between the doorframe and the door. It seemed to take Kyle entirely too long to realize why it wouldn't shut.

"Step back, please," he said.

"It's about Garrett Nelsen," I said, and he promptly stopped trying to force the door to close.

"Why am I not surprised?" he asked. Then he just let go of the door and walked away, toward the backroom where he had apparently been napping.

Andrew and I lunged in through the door and shut it behind us. The shop was all bare shelves, some of them not even entirely assembled yet. A new cash register sat wrapped in plastic on the counter, and the floor was littered with discarded twist-ties and cut packing straps.

"Kyle?" I called as I crossed the empty store to stand in the doorway to the backroom. Kyle was just working his way around a desk whose surface was littered with papers. Bills, I realized when I looked more closely. Past-due stamps abounded.

"As you can see, Garrett Nelsen isn't here," Kyle said, then saw where I was looking and hastily started piling up the bills and jamming them unceremoniously into a drawer.

"No, he wouldn't be," I said.

Kyle threw up his hands in frustration as he collapsed back into his office chair. "You've got that right." But then he looked at me again. "Who did you say you were with? One of the buyers?"

"No, nothing like that," I said. "I'm Ingrid Torfa, and this is Andrew Swanson." Andrew raised a hand to acknowledge his name.

"Okay," Kyle drawled. "Those names mean nothing to me, sorry. Look, I'm sure whatever issue you have with Garrett, that you're totally in the right and something should be done. You're not alone. Oh, no, you're very far from alone." He trailed off with a humorless chuckle.

"Are lots of people looking for Garrett?" Andrew asked.

"He owed a lot of people money," Kyle said, staring down at his hand rubbing at a scuff on the corner of his desk as if it were the most engrossing thing in the world. "A lot of people."

"Angry people?" I asked.

"Some of them," he said, still rubbing at the scuff mark. "They're going to be even angrier now, that's for sure. Did he owe you two money? Because you should know, the way things look now, you're never going to get it. And the business here is a bust before it even started, so there's no point in suing us. Without Garrett, this place is worthless. All of my seed money just went up in smoke. I'll be waiting tables again by the end of the week."

"You know he's dead, then?" I asked.

"Yes," he said. "I got called this morning. Then the police came by to ask me some questions. So I'm well aware."

"You had an alibi?" Andrew asked.

"Not that it's any of your business, but yes," Kyle said, finally looking up with red-rimmed eyes to glare at Andrew. "I was filling in for a sick worker at my parents' café. Lots of witnesses. What's it to you?"

"We're friends of the family," Andrew said, lifting his hands to show he meant no offense. "We're just trying to understand all this. It seems like Garrett had a whole life no one ever knew about."

"More than one," Kyle scoffed. "I knew he had a hustle going on, but I figured once we got the shop running it would be legit. But I'm starting to think he had some other, more dangerous side hustles."

"What hustle?" I asked.

Kyle laughed that humorless laugh again. "Okay, I'll tell you. What does it matter now? The business is tanked, and there's nothing I can do to save it now. But maybe you don't want to tell the family. I don't know." ——

"Tell them what?" I pressed.

"Garrett Nelsen was no artist," Kyle said. "He didn't make any of the things he's been selling."

"Who did?" I asked.

"I don't know," Kyle said. "I wish I did. If I could find that guy and work directly with him, I might have a chance at saving this shop, you know? Now all I have are these whistles. Boxes and boxes of them."

"What are they for?" I asked. "Promotion?"

"I guess," Kyle said. "They were Garrett's idea. But honestly, it makes no sense to me. The art speaks for itself, right?" He barked out another laugh. "The best part is there's probably an unpaid bill in one of these drawers. I owe some manufacturing firm a bunch of money for whistles I'll never be able to sell."

"You should get a lawyer to help you with all this," Andrew said.

"Yeah, because I can afford that," Kyle said.

"You said something about a side hustle?" I prompted.

"Oh," Kyle said, as if he had forgotten his own words. "Well, that's maybe just suspicion on my part. I mean, I thought this was his work we were going to sell here up until just a few days ago. I guess that betrayal still burns. But someone who lies about one thing probably lies about another, right?"

"Maybe," I said. "But do you know anything specific? Anyone else he associated with or maybe you have a paperwork trail?" I looked over the desk, but the remaining papers seemed to largely be doodles, rejected logo designs.

"No, we weren't actually all that close," Kyle said. "We met one day when he was eating at my parents' café and I was waiting on him. We got to talking about business opportunities. I had been saving up my tips since I started working at fifteen, and I had been looking into getting a business loan to start something of my own, not food-related. So I guess I had the business knowledge, but no idea what I really wanted to sell. And Garrett had something to sell, but no business. It felt like a perfect fit. But I guess I never really knew him. He kept to himself, like, a lot. So, no, I never saw him with anyone else or knew of any of his other contacts. But he was always busy, always needed time to get back to me on anything because he had other things cooking. I wished I had asked more questions. I suppose the police will."

"Surely," Andrew said. "But, you know, some people just prefer to be alone most of the time. There might not have been anything there but what it seemed. You might not have been wrong about him."

"I would maybe agree, but he was lying to me about making the art," Kyle said. "I'm sorry, man, all bets are off. All I know is, art doesn't seem like it's worth killing for. I mean, look at me. I just lost everything I've been working for since I was a kid. And I'm angry about it, sure. But I wouldn't kill someone over it. It must've been something else. That's what my gut is telling me, anyway."

I looked over at Andrew, and I could see we were thinking the same thing.

Our guts agreed with Kyle's. Which meant this was another dead end.

CHAPTER 18

I drove back to Runde and parked the car in the back of the meeting hall parking lot. But after switching off the engine, I just sat there.

I had no idea what to do next.

"Ingrid?" Andrew said, putting a hand on my arm, and I realized I was clutching the steering wheel so tight my knuckles were white. I relaxed my grip.

"I'm okay," I said.

"Are you?" he asked. "You're taking this all so personally, and I really don't understand why. You never met Garrett before. You don't know his family. Heck, I barely know his family, despite what we keep telling people."

"I know," I said. "It's just-" But I didn't know how to finish that thought. Not in a way that Andrew could understand. If I told him I was worried about living up to my grandmother's example, I had no idea what that would even mean to him.

"You were upset about Lisa too," he said. "Which was understandable. You nearly hit her with your car. I can get how that might feel personal."

"It was more than that," I said.

"I'm seeing that now," he said. Then he turned to face me. Not easy to do for a man of his height in my little Volkswagen, but he managed it. But I could tell he wanted to look me in the eyes before he said the next thing. "Don't feel like you have to answer, okay? But I'm just wondering if there's something in your past, some reason why this sort of thing seems like a trigger to you."

"You mean like, did I know someone who was murdered?" I asked, and he nodded. "No. My dad died in a car accident, and my mother had a terminal illness. Different kinds of tragedies. I don't think I'm triggered."

"I didn't mean that in a bad way," he said. "You're trying to help people. That's a good thing."

"Part of it is I want to feel like I belong here," I said, which was true, although he only knew half of what I meant by "here."

"You belong," he said. "I suppose our Scandinavian reserve seems pretty cold to a city girl."

I laughed. "They have that in St. Paul too, you know. It takes time to make friends in a new place. But that's not what I'm talking about. I mean, I met you and Jessica and Michelle and Luke in the first five minutes I was here, and I consider you all friends."

"Likewise," he said.

"Anyway, I promised my grandmother I'd check in with her, and she's probably setting up the meeting hall for tonight," I said.

"Okay, sure," he said. "I should get back to the garage before the other boat builders turn up. But if you need anything, text me?"

"You bet," I said.

There was no sign of my grandmother inside the meeting hall, which was still in its drab small town rural building in dire need of upgrades look.

But, to my surprise, Loke was there, leaning against the bar as if he had been waiting for me.

"Where's mormor?" I asked.

"Down in the cellar tinkering with the mead," he said.

"And you're waiting here because..." I said leadingly.

"I'll admit it. I was curious," he said. "I'm betting you didn't just drop this investigation when the Villmark connection didn't pan out."

"No, I didn't," I said. I went behind the bar and turned on the electric kettle my grandmother kept there. Then I scrounged around for mugs and tea.

"I already said I was curious," he said as he watched me work. "Are you going to make me beg?"

"There's nothing to tell," I said. "I've been wandering around following up nothing but dead ends. I guess it's just a matter for the police."

"You don't sound like you really believe that, though," he said. "You've got something wiggling in your gut that says otherwise, don't you?"

"First of all, ew," I said. "But, yeah. I feel like I'm missing something. But without knowing any actual magic, there isn't anything more I can do."

"Did you try any magic?" he asked. The kettle behind me beeped, and I poured steaming hot water into the two mugs, then set one in front of Loke. "Did you?" he pressed.

"I tried to try," I said. "I was in Garret Nelsen's apartment. The police had taken everything that was actual evidence, but I was hoping I would see something."

"How did you try?" he asked.

"Well, the way my grandmother taught me," I said. "To open up my senses and not think and just notice stuff."

"And that works?" he asked with a quirk of his eyebrow.

"Sometimes," I said defensively. "Not today, apparently."

"You didn't do anything more active, then?" he asked, then sipped at his tea.

"Like what?" I asked, exasperated. "All I've been learning is sensing things, and I have no idea if I'm even getting any better at it."

"Nonsense," Loke said. "I heard what you did with the ship."

"That was just an impulse," I said.

"That's what I'm telling you," Loke said. "You need to listen less to your grandmother and more to your own little impulses."

"Where is my grandmother?" I asked, looking towards the door down to the cellar. "She should be here to hear you tell me not to listen to her. She'd just love that."

"All I'm saying is that, clearly, how your grandmother accesses her power is different than how you do it," Loke said with a shrug.

"Is that all you're saying?" I asked.

"She already knows that's true, whether she's said so or not," Loke said. "I bet she's just waiting for you to figure that out on your own."

"If I'm supposed to figure that out on my own, why are you telling me?"

"Rule breaker," he said, pointing a thumb back at himself.

"Yet not a helper," I said and took a sip of tea.

"I'm helping," he said, sounding hurt.

"How are you helping?"

"Well, you're not making it easy," he said with a pout. Then he leaned forward to speak closer to me. "You already know what you wanted to do, but I'm guessing you didn't do it. What was your impulse in Garrett's apartment?"

"I wanted to clear my mind and sense what the space around me wanted to tell me," I said.

"That was a thought, not an impulse," Loke said. "What was your there and gone in a flash impulse?"

I sighed, looking down at my tea. "I wanted to draw. But I didn't have my stuff with me."

"So draw now," he said.

"Draw what?" I asked, leaving aside that I still didn't have my stuff with me. "His parents are probably home by now. I can't sneak back in."

"You're consulting the powers of the universe," Loke said with an eye roll. "You don't have to be in his apartment for that to work."

"I need to focus on *something*," I said. He raised both of his eyebrows and waited for me to figure out what he was thinking. He held that position past the point it was clear I wasn't getting it, then past the point where he looked completely ridiculous.

Then I leaned forward to take another drink of tea and felt the whistle in my pocket grinding against my hip as I pressed up against the counter.

I pulled it out of my pocket and held it out on my palm, and Loke finally leaned back with a satisfied air.

"This isn't the whistle from the murder scene," I said. "It's one of dozens from a box in his apartment."

"I'll refer you back to my previous statement about the powers of the universe," he said. "Ingy, it doesn't matter. You just need a focus."

"Maybe," I said, but I wasn't convinced.

"If you feel like you need more power, you could always go back to the fire behind the waterfall," he said. "It's the oldest place here, and the heart of our ancestress Torfa's powers. But personally, I don't think you need the help."

"Better too much than too little," I said, and drained the last of my tea. "I have to go get my bag with my art stuff. Will you come with me?"

"To your grandmother's?" he asked.

"To the fire," I said.

"Oh, no," he said, shaking his head. "That's not the place for me. But I think I've done enough good works for one day."

"Come on," I said. "You said you were curious."

"I still am," he said. "But I also have a life."

"Do you?" I asked. "Because if you have a job, I've never seen you doing it."

"Maybe I'm doing it right now," he said, then pushed his empty mug across the bar to me. "I'm off. Good luck with communing with the universe. I'm sure I'll hear all about it later."

And with one last wave and one last diabolical grin, he was gone.

CHAPTER 19

*W*hen I got to my grandmother's cabin I ran straight up the stairs to my bedroom to fetch the bag I had never unpacked from the day before. I glanced inside to be sure the sketchbook and pencils were still in there, then ran back down the stairs, but when I went to fetch my walking stick from the bin by the kitchen door, I saw Mjolner curled up on the kitchen table.

"Get down from there," I said, trying to shoo him away. He lifted his head and opened a solitary eye to give me a suspicious look. "Come on. You know mormor hates it."

He blinked that one eye slowly, as if acknowledging my words. Then he stood up and arched his back in a stretch, as if driving home the point that he was in no hurry to do as I asked. But finally even he couldn't stall any longer, and he jumped down off the table to slink away towards the cellar door.

Who was I kidding? He'd be back on the table the minute I stepped outside. But I could at least remind him of the rules he was breaking occasionally.

I started for the door again, but something was nagging at me. Then Loke's words came back to me, about how I had something wiggling in my gut, and I made a mental ew again.

And yet, wiggling was kind of how it felt.

I had thought the kitchen table had caught my attention because Mjolner was sleeping on it, but was that it? Or had that just been a distraction? But there was nothing on it now but the autumn-themed table runner with its needlework of acorns and leaves, and the wooden bowl of apples that were somehow always fresh, crisp and cool despite never being inside her refrigerator.

It had been a long time since lunch, and I had no idea when I'd have dinner. I grabbed a couple of those apples and stuffed them in my bag.

And then I saw the troll. He was still laying on his back and staring up at the ceiling, just like I had left him so many hours before. I picked him up as well and set him on the top of my bag. He wouldn't quite fit inside, and it was awkward carrying him under my arm, but the minute I had him in my possession that wiggling feeling quieted down.

I took the path that circled around the meeting hall, then climbed the main path up to the waterfall.

Now I had another conundrum. I had seen Loke just let himself in, but was I comfortable doing that?

No. No, I was not.

"What Thor is guarding?" I called.

"Thorbjorn," came the answer almost at once.

"Thorbjorn!" I cried and ran down the open cave to where he sat by the roaring bonfire. "I thought you were going on patrol?"

"Thorulv traded places with me," he said. "Are you going up to Vill-mark alone again?"

"No, actually, this was my destination," I said. "I wanted to try some magic here where it's strongest."

"In that case," he said, and turned to fetch another three-legged stool from the corner of the cavern and set it close to the fire, but not too close. "Will you need anything else?" he asked.

"I don't think so," I said. He was being so felicitous. "Is this part of your job?"

"At the fire, yes," he said. "Although few of us study magic these days."

"Just my grandmother," I guessed.

"And, until recently, Halldis," he said, his face giving a little scrunch of distaste. "I hated leaving her alone here, even if that was what was required of me. It always felt wrong. Now I know why."

"We're safe from her here, right?" I asked.

"Of course," he said. "She cannot touch this place."

"Maybe not here, if it's a place of power," I said, "but I feel like she can touch me, sometimes."

"What do you mean?" he asked.

"I've been dreaming about her," I said. "But they don't feel like they're just dreams."

"She touched your mind with her magic," he said. "That sort of thing leaves a mark."

"So she *can* see me," I said.

"I don't know about that," he said quickly. "You might be feeling those things because you were vulnerable to her before. It would be quite natural to be afraid of that happening again." Then he saw the troll resting on the top of my bag. "You're still carrying him around with you?"

"I feel like there's something I'm missing with him," I said. "I wanted to try sketching him, to see if that gets anything flowing in my mind."

"And you wanted to do that here," Thorbjorn said with a little nod. "I see. Well, I was about to do my rounds through the deeper caves, so you'll be alone here with the flames. Best of luck."

"Thanks," I said, setting the troll on the ground beside me so that the fire would not be behind him when I drew him. I felt a wave of vertigo when I looked at him now. The feeling that the wood was alive and capable of motion was amplified by the dancing flames that cast him in a patchwork of light and shadow. It was hypnotic. I immediately reached for my thickest pencil and started marking out his form in large, dark lines.

I never heard or sensed Thorbjorn leaving that cavern. From the moment I started drawing, there was nothing but the troll in front of me and the feel of paper and graphite under my fingers.

I had drawn hundreds of trolls before, but this one was different than the others. There was kindness in his eyes, and a jaunty sense of style in how he wore his mushroom hat. The muscles of his arms and legs were still hard cords, but he seemed more like a farmer and less like a fighter than the trolls I had drawn before. I could imagine him wandering through the woods, gathering mushrooms and berries to eat, visiting friends, always carefully staying out of the light of the sun, which would turn him to stone at the barest touch...

A scuttle of sound pulled me out of my flow state. The sudden transition was so startling it set my heart racing, and I swiveled my head, looking into all the shadowy places around me to find the source of my sudden sense of alarm.

"It's just me," Thorbjorn said, holding up his hands. He was sitting on his stool, and I knew as I looked at him that he had been sitting there quietly for some time, and I had been tuning him out, lost in my drawing.

"Sorry," I said. "I was caught up."

"Did you learn anything?" he asked.

I sighed. "I don't think so. I think I was just telling myself troll stories while I drew," I said. "I do that a lot. Everything I draw, no matter how small in the scale of the larger illustration, has its own back story."

"But you were using magic now," he said.

"I was going to," I said. "I'm not sure I remembered after I got started drawing. I sort of got swept up."

"That doesn't mean you weren't using magic. What does your drawing tell you?" he asked.

I looked down at the sketch. "Nothing," I said. "There are no runes or patterns here that I can see. I mean, it's a great drawing of a troll. But that's all."

Thorbjorn got up from his stool to take a closer look at my work. "It is at least that," he said. "Perhaps you should try drawing the mark on the bottom of his boot. That was added later. Perhaps that is the real clue."

I nodded and turned my sketchbook to a blank page before tipping the troll over. I traced out the swooping lines of the logo, going over and over the shapes. They felt like the wind and the water of Lake Superior, especially as I had known them the day before when the moon and my grandmother's magic had exerted their maximum influence on the waves. But when I was done, there was nothing more there.

"No help?" Thorbjorn guessed when I stopped drawing with a sigh.

"No help," I said. "There's just one thing left to try, and I'm not optimistic."

"Why not?" he asked.

"Well, I'm pretty sure that the logo carved in the bottom of this troll was done by hand. But this?" I took the whistle out of my pocket and set it on a little rise in the ground. "This was mass produced. And even the logo looks like it was designed by a team. No individuality to it at all."

"But you brought it up here for a purpose," Thorbjorn said.

"There was one like it buried in the creek bank near where the murder happened," I said. "But this isn't the same one. This one was in a box, untouched since it left the factory until I picked it up."

"You brought it for a reason," he said. "You won't know what it means until you try. Do you want me to leave?"

"No, you can stay," I said, flipping to yet another blank page in my sketchbook. "I really don't think anything is going to happen. Today is just not my day."

Then I touched the tip of my pencil to the pad, and it was like an electric shock passed through my whole body. I went rigid, and my brain was full of fireworks, and I lost all sense of the world around me.

But I could feel myself drawing like mad.

CHAPTER 20

I don't know how long I was in that fugue state. But when I came out of it the page under my blackened fingers was all heavy, dark lines, overlapping again and again. I could barely make out the shape of the whistle at all. It was like something a kid possessed by a malign spirit would draw.

"Ingrid?" Thorbjorn asked softly, as if not sure if he should disturb me.

"I'm okay," I told him, brushing sweat-soaked hair off my cheek, then realizing belatedly I had probably just left a streak of graphite all over my face.

"Something happened?" he guessed. He was looking at me with a mixture of awe and fear. But surely that had to be fear *for* me. Thorbjorn wasn't afraid *of* anything, least of all me.

"I didn't think anything would, but I guess it did," I said. "Wow. Imagine if I had tried that on the whistle I wanted to draw. The one that had actually been at the murder scene." I shivered.

"What did you see?" he asked.

"Just now? Nothing. I wasn't even in my head for all this," I said, looking down at my drawing again. "But I think I see something now. Yes, look. The whole thing is a jagged mess at first glance, but now that I'm not trying to see the whistle, I see rune forms everywhere. Do you see them?"

Thorbjorn got up from his stool to look over my shoulder at the drawing. In the flickering firelight it looked like the lines were moving on the page, but whereas with Solvi's carvings this sense of movement was always part of the charm, in my own drawing I found it a bit nauseating. Like I was getting seasick from looking at it.

"Yes, I do see something," he said, reaching past me to point at a part of the drawing without quite touching it. "Something secret. A matter of trade."

"Between partners," I said, pointing to another form. But then I sighed. "But we already knew about that. Garrett did have a secret business partner. They were making these whistles to promote their new business. But we talked to Kyle this afternoon, and I really don't think he did it."

"Kyle?" Thorbjorn asked, looking down at me now instead of the drawing.

"Oh, I forgot to mention," I said. I gave him a brief rundown of the trip to Grand Marais, about the new business and about poor Kyle left alone with all the debts.

"He was angry?" Thorbjorn asked.

"Annoyed, more," I said. "I don't think he was killing angry. I didn't get the sense he was hiding anything from us."

"If you believe he is not the murderer after meeting him, that is good enough for me," Thorbjorn said. "But he must be involved somehow. Look, what do you make of this?" He pointed to a place on the opposite side of the page, closer to the mouthpiece of the whistle and away from the logo.

"There's a lot of overlap," I said, squinting at the shapes. "What do you see?"

"They're overlapping because they're bind runes," he said. "There's no way to tell now which you drew and in what order, although we could rule some runes out if their shapes aren't there. What do you see?"

"I'm seeing runes of creation," I said. "Over and over. But creation must mean Solvi, and Solvi had an alibi."

Thorbjorn settled back onto his own stool and tugged at his beard as he mulled it over. "We didn't verify his alibi. The other part could mean him as well. He was a secret business partner as much as this Kyle fellow. No one in Villmark knew Solvi was meeting with Garrett, and no one in Runde who knew of Villmark was aware of their relationship either."

"I think you're right," I said, running my fingertip over the rune shape that referred to a secret partner. "Solvi makes more sense than Kyle. But his alibi?"

Thorbjorn was stroking his beard again, but paused to give me a long look. "I don't remember seeing him. Do you remember seeing him?"

"No, but I left early," I said. "And you were... quite distracted. You were the center of attention, the last place Solvi would be. Maybe we should find Roarr and ask him. Actually, I have a couple of other questions for Roarr about another matter."

"It would be easier to find your grandmother and ask her," Thorbjorn said.

"Yes," I said and closed my sketchbook to slide it back into my bag. But the minute I stood up, I had a sudden memory that washed over me so vividly I fell back onto the stool.

"Ingrid?"

"Hold on," I said, keeping my eyes scrunched tightly shut. "I'm remembering something."

"From when we were kids?" he asked, hope bright in his voice.

"No, sorry," I said. "Last night." I pressed a hand to my head as I ran the memory through my mind again, like a film clip of a newsworthy event. "We don't need to talk to my grandmother."

"Okay. Why not?"

"I know she saw Solvi," I said, opening my eyes to look at him. "But I know when she saw him. It was just after I left."

"That was early in the evening," Thorbjorn said.

"Yes, but late enough for someone to get off the ship, meet Garrett by the bridge and kill him, then go back to the meeting hall to be seen by enough witnesses," I said.

"You saw him arrive?"

"I saw him go in through the front door, the Runde side of the building, just as I was leaving," I said. "I actually ran into him. I was so tired at the time I sort of forgot it, but I'm sure it was him now."

"He could've stepped outside for all sorts of reasons," Thorbjorn said.

"Do you remember seeing him before that? At any point after we left the ship?" I asked.

"No, but I was, as you said, distracted," he admitted.

"We both saw Roarr," I said. "Solvi wasn't with him when we were talking about Roarr."

"That's true," he said. "It's so little to accuse someone on."

"I'm not saying we arrest him," I said. "I'm just saying, we need to talk to him again."

"Then we shall," he said, pushing himself up onto his feet. "I'll seal the door and then we'll go. But Ingrid, you do realize it's nearly dark?"

"I'll be fine," I promised. As unsettling as the path through the woods to Solvi's house had been in daylight, it was bound to be downright unnerving after sunset. But it had to be done.

And I would have Thorbjorn with me.

CHAPTER 21

I left the little troll behind in the fire cave, but I took my
sketchbook with me. If drawing really was necessary for
me to access my magic, I was going to have to acquire some pocket-
sized journals for on the go. But the messenger bag wasn't so heavy as
all that. Especially compared to all the weapons Thorbjorn was
carrying on his belt and strapped to his back.

"Here," Thorbjorn said, adjusting the strap on my bag so that it
rested against my back rather than on my hip, leaving my hands free.
Then he took my walking stick from me and leaned it against the wall
beside the troll and thrust something else into my hands.

"Thorbjorn? I don't know how to use this," I said, looking at the
short spear I was suddenly holding. It reminded me far too much of
the fishing spear that had been plunged into Garrett's back. And the
image of how he must've died, held down under the water until the
thrashing stopped, turned my stomach.

There was no way I could ever do that.

"It's self-explanatory," Thorbjorn told me. "And it's just in case. If
trouble jumps out at us, your first action should be to get behind me.
And if things take a turn for the worse, run."

"Run away and leave you?" I asked.

"Run away and return with help," he said. "But don't worry. I'm sure it will be fine."

"It's the full moon," I said.

"The extra light will come in handy."

"It's overcast."

"If you want to speak with Solvi, we must go where Solvi is," he said.

"Sure, but can't we bring your brothers?" I asked.

He looked appalled. "Summon all my brothers to escort us on a walk into the woods? And not even very deep into the woods? Just a little stroll outside of the village boundaries? I would never hear the end of it."

"All right," I conceded. "You know the level of danger better than I do. I yield to your experience."

"I'm not going to let anything bad happen to you, Ingrid," he promised.

We trekked through the town and past Thorbjorn's house, cresting the last hill before plunging down into the woods. The sun had only just set, and it wasn't so dark as I had expected under the trees. Still, the quality of all sound being swallowed unheard persisted. I wasn't sure if I wanted to make more noise or less. Did I feel safer when I crept along quietly, or when I made a racket to announce my approach?

It didn't seem to make any difference to the forest. And I didn't think any sound I made carried past more than a tree or two.

We reached Solvi's hut far sooner than I was expecting it. As we emerged from the trees, the clouds parted to let the full moon rising over the hill behind us shine down into the clearing. The scattering of statues had an eerie quality in the gloaming that became downright sinister when lit by the brightness of the moon. Its silvery light lit up one side of everything nearly as bright as day, but thrust the other side into even deeper shadow.

"It doesn't look like anyone's home," I whispered to Thorbjorn as we approached the green door. The windows to either side were dark, and there was no smell of smoke from the chimney or sound of anyone moving about within. Still, Thorbjorn knocked loudly and called out Solvi's name.

"This is my fault," I said.

"What do you mean?"

"He's probably back at the mead hall with my grandmother and everyone else," I said. "I could've saved us a lot of walking if we'd just checked there first."

"Maybe," Thorbjorn said. "But I don't think so. Two nights in a row in the mead hall? That's not like Solvi."

"Does it make him look guilty?" I wondered. "Trying to shore up his alibi or something?"

"If he ran off on us, it would certainly make him look guilty," Thorbjorn said darkly.

"We should see if he's with the others before we condemn him," I said.

"Well, we came all the way out here," Thorbjorn said, and he turned the door handle. It stopped abruptly, clearly locked, but Thorbjorn just turned it further. I heard a snap of metal and then the door was swinging open.

"That's the first locked door I've seen since coming up north," I said. "Although he does live pretty far out of town. Does he lock it for protection, do you think?"

"To keep out the bears who've mastered doorknobs?" Thorbjorn asked me, then plunged into the darkness within the hut. I hovered near the doorway while he poked the fire in the fireplace back to life, then used its flame to light the lantern that rested on the mantle.

I was going to come in when it was no longer dark and I was sure of not tripping over anything, but the moment the light bathed everything I was dumbstruck in the doorway.

And I had thought the woodworking was gorgeous on the outside. That had all been just hints of waves in the flow of the boards, brought out by a few carved touches and careful use of stain. But inside? The inside was so much more.

Everything around me had a fanciful touch. There was an elabo-

149

rate knot work carved into the wood beams, then colored red, blue and gold to bring out the pattern. The bed was a mattress resting inside an ornate wooden box, carved all over with running wolves chasing the sun and the moon over and over again, in a dozen subtly different ways. The fireplace had carvings in nine distinct groupings, which I quickly realized represented the nine worlds of Norse creation stories.

But most glorious of all was the central beam. Branches with leaves were carved all over it, but near the floor I could see a dragon chewing at exposed roots and a trio of women gathered around a pool of water. I looked up to see a little squirrel racing up one of the leafy branches at about my eye level. Then I tipped my head back to see the top of the beam opened out into a delicately carved leafy canopy, and among those carved branches an eagle was perched, perfectly positioned to watch me standing in the doorway.

"It's Yggdrasil," I said. "Oh my goodness, this place is gorgeous."

"You're just scratching the surface," Thorbjorn said as he continued to feed branches to the fire, adding ever more light to the cabin's interior. "Open the doors on the cupboard in the kitchen and you'll see scenes of farm-life, our ancestors and some of their Ojibwe companions. Lie back on the bed and look up at the ceiling, and you'll see the ship that brought our ancestors here at the moment of Torfa's spell. You can tell lake from sea in the carving, it's so intricate. And the bathtub in the other room is all carved wood as well, showing the Valkyries flying into battle for some reason. He's probably added some things since I was here last."

I started towards the door to the bathroom, but stopped myself. We were there for a reason, and admiring the art wasn't that reason. "There's no creek near here, is there? No reason for him to have a fishing spear."

"No, and I've never noticed one here before," Thorbjorn said. He turned to close the door behind me. Behind where the open door had stood was a rack that held assorted tools, not for woodworking save perhaps for the axe, but for farming. There was no hook without a tool hanging from it, but there was something like an umbrella stand that was empty. "His walking stick is gone," Thorbjorn said as if he had followed my gaze.

"Is anything else missing?" I wondered, turning to look on the other side of that gorgeous bed. I threw back the lid on the chest that formed a seat under the window, but there was nothing inside of it.

"His clothes," Thorbjorn said, looking over my shoulder at the empty chest. "His weapons. His cloak, which should be on that peg there."

"He would need that to get to the mead hall. It's chilly out there. And a lot of you Villmarkers wear your weapons all the time. Especially walking through the woods, which he would've had to do."

"Ingrid, he took all his clothes," Thorbjorn said, sweeping his hand towards the empty chest. "He packed up his things, as much as he could carry, and he left."

I sank down on the edge of the bed. "He's looking guilty, isn't he?" I sighed. "Or else he's worried about my grandmother knowing he was selling art on the sly. Maybe that's what he's running from."

"I don't think so," Thorbjorn said. He opened the door again and leaned out into the night. "I see no sign of which way he might have gone, and even with the moon it's too dark for me to track him through the woods."

"So what do we do?" I asked.

"Wait until morning," he said, and closed the door.

There were worse things in the world than passing a night in a cozy little cabin with Thorbjorn, especially when he walked over to the kitchen and took out a heavy loaf of rye bread and a wheel of cheese. That would go perfectly with the apples I had in my bag.

But if Solvi really was running away and hadn't just gone to the mead hall or some place in Villmark, then every moment we delayed made it less and less likely that we'd ever find him again.

And I had to know what happened. I wouldn't believe that someone who could create such wonderful art, art that seemed to be bestowed with its own spark of life, could murder someone the way Garrett had been murdered. It just didn't make any sense.

151

But if Thorbjorn couldn't track him through the woods at night, what choice did we have but to wait?

I laid back on the bed and found myself looking up at the carving of a ship with its front end in Lake Superior and its back end in the North Sea. Thorbjorn was right. Even in the dim light that reached inside the bed frame, you could totally tell he was depicting two different bodies of water. It was like a magical illusion.

I sat back up, shoving the pillows against the headboard to support me as I pulled my sketchbook out of my bag and set it on my drawn-up knees.

I knew what to do. But would it work here, so far from the magic fire?

I thought it would. This cabin was filled with a different sort of magic, maybe a less powerful kind, but a kind I was far more attuned to.

My first few strokes were slow, uncertain, but as the curves began to define a shape, I grew more confident and worked faster. I was vaguely aware of Thorbjorn saying something to me, but his words couldn't reach my furiously active mind. I felt my fingers pressing harder, making more aggressively dark lines. That wasn't my usual style, but then I was blending the graphite under my thumb. Just like I had done when I had drawn the waterfall parting for the ship.

This was how I did it. This was how I accessed my magic.

Thorbjorn sat down on the edge of the bed and the mattress gave way, sending me rolling enough to shift the sketchbook off my knees.

"Sorry!" he said. "I just wanted to see what you were doing."

"Look," I said, handing him the sketchbook.

"Solvi," Thorbjorn said appreciatively. "You drew his face from memory?"

"More than that," I said, "look at his hair."

Thorbjorn tipped the sketchbook to catch the light, then got up from the bed to carry it closer to the lamp on the mantle. "Are those mountains?"

"Yes!" I said. "I saw it, saw it as I was drawing it. Do those mountains look familiar? Does it mean anything?"

Did I *do* anything?

Thorbjorn continued examining my drawing without speaking, and my heart began to sink. But then he turned to me and there was a twinkle in his eye. "Yes. I know this place. It's not far from here. It must be where Solvi intends to go, and that's why you drew it in his head like this."

"I don't think the position on the page is important," I started to say, but this was no time to argue artistic intent. "Never mind. We have to get there, right away."

"But Ingrid, this is further into the woods. Dangerously further into the woods."

"Well, there isn't time to take me back to Villmark first and then for you go out to get him on your own," I said. "I could feel as I was drawing him that he's getting further and further away. There really isn't much time."

"You could wait here," Thorbjorn said. "You'd be perfectly safe, and I would bring him straight here for you. You could ask him all of your questions."

"Thanks for the offer," I said, "but I really think the only plan is for me to go with you."

"Ingrid," he started to say with a shake of his head, but I didn't let him finish.

"Look again at the mountains in that picture," I said, scrambling off the bed to show him. "This mark here, nearly through this mountain pass? That's Solvi."

"Okay," Thorbjorn said.

"And these two down here," I said, pointing to the very bottom of the mountain image, at what was more hair than landscape, "these are us. You and me."

"But you drew this," he said. "And you weren't all swept up like before. You drew this with intent. You drew yourself here because you wanted to go."

"I did," I agreed. "And that intent hasn't changed. Put it this way. Do you want to leave with me now and go after Solvi, or do you want to argue about it first and *then* leave with me to go after Solvi?"

"Well, if you put it that way," Thorbjorn said and thrust my sketch-book back into my arms.

"I do put it that way," I said. "Now, let's go."

CHAPTER 22

*A*fter banking down the fire in Solvi's fireplace, we went back out into the night.

The moon had left the sky, and the sculptures dotted around the clearing were no more than formless shadows against the grayish-black of the forest beyond. We circled the cottage and crossed the dried remains of the kitchen garden, then pressed on to the far side of the clearing where the little forest path resumed.

The path started climbing almost at once, up and around one hill after another. The trees were denser here, their branches intertwined just over our heads as if we were inside a living tunnel. But even though everything was pressed close around us, the soundscape had opened up wide. My steps on the needle-strewn ground were the appropriate volume, but other sounds around us were amplified. They echoed without fading. I had no idea whether the acorn I heard plummet to the ground was a foot away from me or on the far side of the valley.

I clutched the short spear that Thorbjorn had given me and tried not to jump at every sound around us. But from the way Thorbjorn kept looking over at me, I don't think I was succeeding.

"It's all right, Ingrid," he told me. But as if to prove him wrong, there was a sudden rush of sound off to our left. It was like a boulder rolling down the hillside, smashing through the trees.

"What was that?" I asked. I wanted to scream, but I didn't dare speak above a whisper.

"Probably nothing," he said.

"I don't believe you," I said.

"Look, anything making that much noise is probably just a bear," he said.

"Just a bear?" I asked. "*Just* a bear?"

"Yes, just a bear," he repeated. "The giants are smart enough to pick their way through the less dense parts of the forest, if they should happen to be out at night, which they almost never are. And even a troll knows how to be sneakier than that. No, that was almost definitely a bear."

"There could be trolls here?" I asked.

"Perhaps," he said with a shrug.

"And they might attack us?"

"Only if there were a large number of them," he said with a slight raise of his axe.

"And they would be sneaking?"

"If they knew what was good for them," he said.

"So you're telling me that I should be more afraid of the things I *can't* hear?" I asked.

"Well-"

"And that there almost definitely is a bear just a few feet away from us?" I went on.

"He wasn't just a few feet away," Thorbjorn said. "He was at least one hill over, and anyway that's stopped now."

"So we're back to things lurking out there that don't make such a racket?" I asked.

"I never should've let you talk me into taking you along," he said.

"No, I'm fine," I said. "I just want to understand the risks. You said we came here all the time as kids, but I just don't remember it."

"We didn't go this far in as kids," he said gravely. Then a hint of a grin twitched at the corner of his mouth. "Well, just that one time, but we got in so much trouble we never did it twice."

"I need to relearn what I learned then," I said as we resumed our climb up the hill. "And there is so much new stuff to learn after that."

"We have time," he said. "But if we're going to be coming out here a lot, we're going to have to start with some weapons training. That little spear isn't going to do you much good against real trouble."

"Oh, thanks," I said. "Why am I carrying it again?"

"To make you feel better?"

"Well, it's all I have now. I don't think I can run back for help from here," I said, looking back down the way we'd come.

"Just follow the path," Thorbjorn said. "You wouldn't have to get all the way home, or even all the way back to Solvi's house."

"Why not?" I asked.

"Because we've already crossed into the deeper realms. My brothers know we are here," he said. "Any of the five of us can sense it when one of us goes this deep."

"But you've gone deeper than this before?" I asked.

He stopped abruptly, and I realized we had reached the far edge of the forest. The trees didn't taper out, they just ended all in a line. But there were no stumps anywhere to suggest they were cut down for lumber. There was nothing more than bare rock and some kind of dried ground cover I didn't recognize except to know that it wasn't like the usual grass of northern Minnesota.

"You've been deeper than this?" I asked again. Thorbjorn turned to look at me, and there was something inscrutable in his eyes.

"Two of my brothers have," he said. "But not I."

"Why did Solvi come this way if it's a place even you five don't go?"

"That is a question I'd like to ask him myself," Thorbjorn said, then led the way further up the hillside.

The hill was steeper here, and far rockier. But these weren't the glacier-smoothed rock faces of the North Shore. These were jagged, sharp, and even in the poor light of the mostly overcast night, they looked darkly volcanic.

"Where are we?" I asked, scanning the horizon behind us for any sign of the lake. I could just see water off to the east, reflecting a bit of light that wasn't reaching us on the hillside. "This doesn't look like Minnesota, but I don't think it looks like Norway either. It's like Iceland?"

"That's one theory," Thorbjorn said. "That is where Torfa was trying to take her people. Parts of it could've been caught up in her spell, even though that's not where the people ended up."

Then he caught my sleeve, indicating we should rest for a moment against one of the larger boulders. I wasn't going to argue with that. It was hard enough work climbing the hill without also trying to talk, and I was quite out of breath. I turned to rest my backside against a protrusion of rock and looked back over the lake.

Or was it the lake? If we were in a sort of Iceland, might it be the ocean I was looking at? How could I know? Either would reach the horizon.

I was about to ask Thorbjorn about the other theories when there was a sudden skittering of pebbles sliding down over a rock-face. We both turned and peered around the boulder towards the top of the hill.

But it wasn't just one hill. It was two. I had been so focused on where I put my feet as we climbed and in looking back towards the lake or whatever that I had never looked where we were going. But I recognized it now.

We were standing just where I had drawn us in my sketch of Solvi, and towering over us was a pair of hills. The path gleamed dully in the cloud-obscured moonlight, but I could pick it out as it wound its way through a pass between those two hills.

And scrambling up that path, just about to disappear between two immense boulders that flanked the path like sentinels, was a dark figure I just knew was Solvi.

"He's getting away!" I hissed to Thorbjorn, but it's not like he needed me to tell him that. He made a vague motion for me to stay where I was, but didn't wait for me to acknowledge it before he started racing up the hillside.

You would never guess he'd been winded just a moment before, not to judge by the speed he was climbing that hill.

I heard another skittering of rock, and at first I thought it was coming from under Thorbjorn's feet as he churned things up. But then I saw Thorbjorn throw an arm across his eyes as if to ward off a blow and realized it was coming from higher up.

Was Solvi creating a landslide?

I looked back up towards the pass, but Solvi was no longer in view.

And yet I could hear rocks raining down from above. Some hit other rocks and smashed in an explosion of shards, others buried themselves in the softer earth like a shot put thrown by an Olympic athlete.

But most were striking Thorbjorn. The bracers on his arms were protecting him from the smaller rocks that were pelting him, but if one of the larger ones should fail to miss?

He must've had the same thought I did, because he turned and ran back to the protection of our boulder.

"Something is up there!" I said, trying to peek around the side of the boulder. There were shadows, so many shadows, and yet my eyes wouldn't bring them into focus in the poor light.

Then Thorbjorn grabbed the back of my windbreaker and yanked me down to sit beside him. I was about to object when one of the larger rocks struck the boulder above me, showering us both with rock shards, and I had to cover my eyes with my hands.

"He got through the pass. He's getting away!" I said to Thorbjorn.

"No, he isn't," Thorbjorn said with iron resolve.

"But there's something up there throwing these rocks at us," I said. "This is no rockslide."

"No, it's trolls," he said.

"There must be dozens of them!" I said as more rocks struck the ground all around us. We were safe, providing they didn't leave the ridge.

And I didn't think they would. They seemed to be pinning us down to buy Solvi time to escape.

"Maybe twelve," Thorbjorn said, brushing at his face then frowning at the blood that was smeared across his hand. One of those stones had hit him just by the hairline, but he pulled away before I could take a closer look at it.

"We should go back," I said.

"No," he said, shifting his weight so that he could reach something at the back of his belt. His axe? His sword? What good would they do against rock-wielding trolls who were so far away? Maybe if one of us had a bow, although in the time it took to aim, we'd probably have our heads smashed in.

"What else can we do?" I asked. "He knew we were after him, and he rounded up his troll friends. He beat us."

"No!" Thorbjorn said. "This isn't over."

Then he got up on one knee. I reached out to hold him back, thinking he was going to try to run up the hill again, but he wasn't facing the right away for that. He was facing back behind us, back towards Villmark.

And what he had taken from his belt was not a weapon. It was a horn. He brought it to his lips and blew a single blast of sound.

The whole world stood still while that sound rang out around us, echoing over the hills and carrying through the forest below. It was like every creature in this between-world space was holding its breath at that clear tone until Thorbjorn's lungs gave out and the sound faded away.

For a moment, nothing happened. Nothing at all. Everything was still and quiet.

And then the rocks were raining down on us once more.

CHAPTER 23

I looked longingly back down the hill towards the forest. The trees that had been so darkly ominous moments before were looking like a haven of safety to me now.

They also looked about a million miles away. And the ground between where Thorbjorn and I sat and the tree line was getting pounded by rock after rock.

We couldn't go back. But we couldn't go forward either. Solvi was getting away, but that had become a minor point now. How were *we* going to get away?

"I'm going to divert their attention," Thorbjorn said to me. He had his sword in one hand and his axe in the other.

"What? Why?" I asked.

"So you can get away," he said. "Run, back down the path. Don't stop until you reach Villmark."

"I'm not leaving you," I said.

"You'll be perfectly safe," he said.

"That's not what I'm talking about and you know it!" I said. I shifted my position to pull my messenger bag onto my lap. "There must be something I can do. Something I can draw to help us."

But even as I dug through the bag for my sketchbook, I didn't know what that could be. Or how I would see to do it. The clouds between us and the moon were getting thicker by the minute.

"Ingrid, you have to go," Thorbjorn said. "I'll be fine."

"I don't believe you," I said.

"My brothers will be here-" But then he broke off, squinting down at the trees below us.

And then he started to smile, a wide, crazy smile. It was almost frightening, that smile.

"What is it?" I asked, gazing down the hill. Then I saw it. Something was moving through the trees.

No, several somethings. I scanned the top of the forest and saw four distinct lines where the leaves were shaking as if the trees themselves were being pushed out of the way only to snap back into place.

Then they burst out of the trees, four dark silhouettes. All I could tell in the dim light was that they were tall, and they were carrying weapons. They paused for a moment as if getting their bearings, then raised their weapons into the air with a mighty yell.

I nearly jumped out of my skin as that yell was echoed right beside me. Thorbjorn was on his feet, sword and axe thrust into the air, hair blowing wildly around him as he bellowed up towards the sky.

Man, I hoped these were his brothers.

"We fight!" Thorbjorn called, and the four below roared back. Then he bent down to speak to me, his voice calmer but his eyes still wild, "stay here."

Before I could answer, he was gone, launching over the top of the boulder and disappearing up the hillside.

I stayed where I was, pressing back against the rock as the four silhouettes below also raced up the hill. They drew ever closer, swords and axe blades flashing in the light as the moon found little gaps in the cloud cover.

Then the moon burst free, bathing the hillside in silvery light, and I saw all of Thorbjorn's brothers as clear as day. They looked like him, with the same oversized build and strawberry-blond hair. But there were differences.

One had his head shaved on the sides, with intricate blue tattoos tracing out a knot work pattern that arced over his ears. He had a short sword like a Roman legionnaire would use, but the axe in his other hand was massive.

Another had no beard and short, spiky hair and carried two curved knives.

The third had his hair divided into three thick braids, and his beard was divided into two braids. He had a spear in his hands, the shaft so thick and heavy it seemed impossible it could be thrown.

The last had shaved all the hair from his head, his scalp and face heavily tattooed with blue ink in a complex pattern I wanted a better look at. His beard was left long, so long that he wore it tucked into the strap that crossed his chest. He had a sword in each hand.

They were past me almost before I could note all those details. With my sketchbook right there on my lap it was difficult not to start sketching them while the images were fresh in my mind, but I could hear Thorbjorn fighting further up the hill, and the roar as his brothers joined him. Now wasn't the time.

I put away the sketchbook and pushed the messenger bag back behind me before risking a peek over the top of the boulder. The trolls had stopped throwing rocks and had come out of their hiding places to close in on the brothers. The trolls weren't so tall as the brothers, but they were possibly more heavily muscled. And they were using those muscles to swing clubs that looked like the trunks of trees. If throwing all those rocks had tired them at all, they weren't showing it.

They outnumbered the brothers by more than four to one, but they were still outmatched. They couldn't use their numbers to good use, tripping over each other and getting in each other's way, and even on more than one occasion braining one another with their clubs. This fight only had one outcome, and it was just a matter of time.

Then a flicker of motion caught my eye, something ducking out of sight in the pass between the hilltops. Solvi? Had he lingered to watch the fight rather than make good his escape?

I gripped my spear and bent low as I ran up the hill, circling the combat as widely as I could before angling back to reach the path between the boulders at the top of the pass.

"Solvi?" I called as I approached the boulders. It felt like a great place for an ambush. But there was no sign of him. Had I imagined it?

Then I heard a skitter of pebbles on rock coming from the path on the far side of the pass. I ran past the boulders to see Solvi jogging away from me.

"Solvi, stop!" I called after him, but he didn't slow down. He didn't speed up either; it was like he was in no particular hurry. Like the idea of being caught didn't strike him as likely enough to worry about.

I remembered my grandmother's command voice, the one she had used that morning to tell the Sorensens and Nelsens to quiet down. Could I do that voice? I had sensed her magic in that moment. There was no way to draw a sound, though. I was going to have to try imitating what she had done.

"Solvi!" I said, and to my surprise I heard something different in my own tone. It was bright and silvery, like a bell in the thin air of a mountaintop village. "Stop!"

He stopped. He really did. I knew I was grinning like a fool, but I had earned the right to be a little proud of myself, hadn't I?

"Solvi, come back!" I said in that same magical voice.

But Solvi only turned to look up at me. He didn't come back. Then he gave me a little bow. It looked genuinely solemn, not like he was mocking me. And yet, when he spoke, all he said was, "I regret that I must decline."

And then he was jogging down the hillside path again. I had failed.

"Thors!" I called, a bit startled to hear I was still doing the magic voice. I wasn't sure how to turn it off.

But it wasn't working on them either. I could hear the fight continuing, even as I could hear the sound of Solvi's footsteps getting ever further away. I went back between the boulders to look down the slope of the hill to where the battle raged on.

The brothers were clearly having the time of their lives, sending troll after troll tumbling down the hill. But the trolls at the bottom of the hill were shaking themselves off, reaching for their fallen clubs or

DEATH UNDER THE BRIDGE

uprooting a tree to make another, and charging back up to rejoin the fight.

This could go on all night. But I really needed them to stop and listen to me.

I had a magic voice like my grandmother's, but that was not enough. A large measure of why my grandmother had gotten the response that she had was that the people of Runde, like the people of Villmark, already respected her. She didn't need to magically make that part happen. And if she needed their attention in a hurry, she only needed to give them a little magical nudge, since they were inclined to listen to her anyway.

Me, on the other hand? I was a long way from getting that level of respect from anyone. I hadn't earned it yet.

I wished my grandmother were there, but it was nowhere near midnight. And until midnight passed, she would be tied up in the meeting hall, maintaining the spells that held that impossible community together. I was on my own.

I was clearly not ready to take up the mantle of a volva. And yet that was what I had to do, or else Solvi was going to slip away to where no one would ever find him again. Not the Thors. Not even my grandmother.

I slumped down on a rock, but one thought kept me from slipping into a dejected funk.

The mantle of volva.

That was how I had phrased it a moment ago. And in fact my grandmother had an actual mantle she wore for official occasions, a cloak of feathers and a bronze wand both. Those things were miles away, back in Villmark, back in that entirely different world.

But maybe there was a way around that.

I took out my sketchbook again and turned to a blank page. Then I began to draw. I wasn't swept up in a furious flow of creativity. It felt like work the entire time, but it was work I knew well.

I sketched out myself, sitting on a rock much like the rock I was sitting on as I drew. But the me on the rock was wearing a magnificent cloak of feathers. Not ancient and worn like my grandmother's, but fresh and new. Even in the pencil sketch, they had a glow to them like they were from some golden hawk.

And I put a wand in my hand, a wand the size of a sword. And that wand was radiating power as sketch-me held it aloft.

When I could think of no more details to add I looked up, then raised my pencil overhead as if it were that sword-wand.

"Stop the fighting!" I said. My voice still had the quality of bells to it, but these were fearsome bells. Massive call-to-war bells.

The Thors didn't react at all.

But the trolls did. And when every troll threw down their club to plop down on the dried grass of the stony hillside, the Thors lost all of their combat partners. Then they too lowered their weapons and turned their attention to me.

"Thors," I said, and this time I was speaking in my normal voice once more. "Solvi is getting away. You need to go catch him."

They looked at me blankly for a moment, all five of them breathing too hard to speak. But then they nodded and ran past me, down the far side of the hill, after the receding silhouette of Solvi.

CHAPTER 24

*A*s I watched Thorbjorn and his brothers catch up with the still-jogging figure of Solvi down in the valley below, I sensed movement around me. The trolls were still sitting on the dried grass, but they were scooting closer until they were sitting all around me, watching me with open, if ugly, faces. They were like children at some library's story time, and they were all waiting for me to start reading them the story.

"Do you know who I am?" I asked them.

"You are the volva," one of them said, and gestured as if at something around me. They were still seeing me as I had drawn myself, I guessed. I adjust the ends of my windbreaker, to let it drape a bit more like that cape.

"That's true, but you can call me Ingrid," I said to the trolls.

"Ingrid," they all chorused, nodding as if my name confirmed their suspicions about me.

"Why were you helping Solvi escape?" I asked.

"Escape?" They looked at each other to see if any of them knew what I meant.

"There has been a murder. Thorbjorn and I wanted to talk to Solvi. But then he ran away, and you were helping him escape," I said.

"Solvi is our friend," one of them said, and then they were all nodding their agreement with that fact.

"So he ordered you to stop us from following him?" I asked.

"Ordered? No," the one in front said. "Solvi is our friend. He asked."

"And we helped," another said. "Because Solvi is our friend."

"Yes, I understand that bit," I said.

"But also, fighting the Thors is fun," the first troll said, and the others laughed and offered their hearty ascent to this assessment.

"Ingrid!" Thorbjorn called, and I turned to see him coming back up the hill, his brothers with Solvi following behind.

"Good, you've got him," I said, and resisted the urge to fuss with my windbreaker again. I wasn't sure if they saw me as volva or not, but trying to adjust anything was more likely to break an illusion than to help it. Then I realized I was still holding my pencil like a wand and put my hands on my lap.

"Sorry, we got caught up," he said when he'd reached my side. He had put his weapons away and was mopping the blood and sweat from his brow with the edge of his cloak. Then he looked back to watch the others approach. "Ingrid, may I present my brothers?"

"Absolutely," I said.

"This is my oldest brother, Thorulv," Thorbjorn said, waving a hand towards the brother with the completely shaved head, who gave me a solemn nod. I returned the gesture.

"My second oldest brother, Thormund," Thorbjorn said, moving his hand to indicate the brother with the multiple thick braids. We also exchanged nods.

"Thorge, my younger brother," Thorbjorn went on, and I nodded to the brother who shaved the sides of his head.

"And finally, my youngest brother, Thoralv," he said, and I nodded to the brother with the short, spiky hair and no beard. He nodded back, as solemn as the others, but then broke into a grin. He looked like he would be just barely out of high school, if Villmark had a high school.

"My thanks to all of you," I said. "And it's good to finally meet you."

"She thought I had made you all up," Thorbjorn said with a laugh.

"After what happened when we were kids?" Thormund asked.

"She doesn't remember that far back," Thorbjorn said, but then added with more cheer in his voice, "not *yet*."

"You are here as volva, then?" Thorulv asked in a grave tone after the laughter of the others had died.

Was I? I had only created that mantle for myself to stop the fighting, and yet, wasn't I about to deal with a matter of justice? That was part of my grandmother's purview.

They were all looking at me with expectant faces. I had to say something. "Really, I just wanted to ask Solvi some questions. But he ran away before I could speak to him, and then he set a troll ambush on us to keep us from following him. So perhaps this *is* an official matter now."

"A matter for the council, perhaps?" Thorulv asked.

I bit my lip. Was I overstepping here?

"Solvi will answer Ingrid's questions now," Thorbjorn said, coming to stand with folded arms behind me. "We were intending to do this in a friendly manner, but Solvi is the one who made that impossible. So now he will answer the same questions, but to a volva. That is just."

"But will his fate be decided here? Will his sentence be carried out here?" Thorulv pressed.

I could feel Thorbjorn about to answer for me, but when I raised my hand, he fell silent. Maybe the Thors weren't as in my thrall as the trolls were, but they were still behaving with more deference than usual. Or at least Thorbjorn was.

"That will depend on his answers to my questions," I said. Thorulv appeared to think this over, but then gave me a nod and took half a step back, yielding the point to me.

"Very well," I said, squeezing my hands together as if I could somehow lend myself strength. "Solvi. What do you have to say for yourself?"

"I will say as much as you like," Solvi said. "I will tell you everything. But I hope in return to ask for one boon."

"That will depend on what you have to say, and on the nature of that boon," I said.

Solvi nodded as if he had expected that to be the answer.

"Tell me what happened with Garrett," I said.

"I met him under the bridge last night," Solvi said. "But perhaps I should start my tale a bit sooner?"

"We already discussed how you were breaking the Villmark rules by selling your art in the modern world, and that Garrett was your distributor," I said. "And I know he was passing that work off as his, and that he had a new partner that was helping him take his business to the next level. You knew all this as well?"

"I discovered it," Solvi said with a nod. "When Garrett Nelsen and I reached our first agreement, he promised me my art would be everywhere. He could sell some of it, we agreed, but some of it must be free for all to see. In museums, in exhibitions, things like that. This is what I wanted. But each of the next three times I met him, it became more clear that Nelsen was interested only in making money. And that a little money made him hungry for more, and more money made him hungrier still."

"You couldn't keep up with the demand?" I asked. I could scarcely believe it. I had seen all that Solvi had done, so many pieces that were being traded and bought and sold, but also the work on his own house and on the Viking ship. I had thought I was a productive artist, but Solvi put me to shame.

"I was not given the opportunity to try," Solvi said, and for the first time an emotion was inflecting his normally stoic voice. He sounded bitter.

"What do you mean?" I asked.

"Nelsen was planning to cheat me," Solvi said.

"How?" I asked.

"I will tell it as I learned of it," Solvi said after a moment's thought. "Yesterday, when we were all on the ship, we saw that new bridge. The steel one."

"Yes," I said. "The Nelsens keep building a bridge there, but the Sorensens keep tearing it down."

"Indeed," Solvi said. "The Nelsens need the bridge to connect their fields, but the Sorensens tear it down because it is too low for their fishing boats to pass under it."

"Hold on," I said, holding up a hand. "Why do the farming Sorensens care about fishing boats?"

"I do not understand you," Solvi said.

"It is an old feud," Thorulv said. "This bridge has been a source of conflict since Runde was founded. But now it is just like a reflex to fight over it. It is possible neither family remembers why, only that they must fight over this bridge as a matter of family honor."

"I suppose originally there weren't fishing Sorensens and farming Sorensens. There were just Sorensens," I said, thinking out loud. "If the bridge really did block the boats from reaching the lake, that could be why half of them moved closer to the shore."

"Also, with your modern trucks and the roads that crisscross the river valley, the bridge is not so important to the Nelsens as it was once, when farming was done with horses or just manpower," Thorbjorn added.

"Yeah," I nodded. "Wow. I can't wait to talk to mormor about this."

Solvi took a deep breath, as if eager to get on with his tale. I waved for him to continue. "On the ship, after we passed the bridge, two of the Villmarkers sitting by me on the rowing benches were talking about that bridge. They drank often with the people of Runde and had heard tales. The bridge was made of steel this time. Harder to burn down, but also far more expensive. But important to the Nelsen family."

"You think Garrett paid for it?" I asked. "With money he made from your art? But you wanted him to sell it. I'm still not sure why this upset you."

"Because," Solvi said, "he didn't earn that money by selling the pieces of my art which I had given him. He made it by selling the art itself."

"I don't follow you," I said.

"He had found a..." he stopped to hunt for the word, then landed with, "manufacturer. Someone who would look at one of my pieces and make thousands of inferior copies."

"Oh," I said. Then I remembered that whistle, and Kyle's suspicion that there were other secret partners that Garrett was meeting with. "Oh," I said again, more slowly.

"This I could not abide," Solvi said, although his voice was as calm as ever. "I sent him a message to meet me at once so that we could discuss it."

"So you met under the bridge," I said.

"No," Solvi said. "That would be too visible. I knew enough about this family quarrel by then to know that the Sorensens would at once need to find a way to tear that bridge down. Even at night, that place would be too exposed to meet Nelsen there. No, we met outside the barn where he claimed to craft my art. As if he ever could." There was that hint of bitterness again.

"Then what?" I asked.

"His parents were home, so that wasn't a safe place to talk either. So we walked closer to the creek. There was a shed there, so old and neglected it was barely still standing. It had once been a fishing house, but had been long since abandoned, being too far from the lake. I confronted Nelsen about his plans, but he didn't even try to deny what he was doing," Solvi said. "He didn't even deny knowing that it wasn't a part of our agreement, or that he knew I would object to it. He just didn't care. Not about our agreement, not about my art, not about anything but money. And he told me he was about to make a lot of money."

"So what did you do?" I asked.

"I demanded that he stop everything," Solvi said. "I demanded that he return to our original agreement and stop all plans for mass producing my work."

"Let me guess," Thorbjorn said. "He said no?"

Solvi nodded. "He said he didn't even need me anymore. He had made copies of everything I had already given him, with some modern technology. He showed me one of these copies on his phone," Solvi said, hesitating only momentarily over the word. "It looked like just lines on a screen to me, but I could see the shape of my work there. He said there was nothing I could do to stop it, that those copies were already in multiple locations." He stopped to take another deep breath, but this one caught in his throat momentarily. "Then he showed me a picture of one of these copies. Not in wood, but in plastic. And it was an abomination."

"So you killed him," Thorbjorn finished for him.

"I killed him," Solvi said without emotion. "There was a fishing spear in that ruin of a shed. Nelsen was laughing and walking away from me as if the discussion were over when it was not. And that spear was in my hand. Then it was in his back."

"Then you put the body in the creek so it would wash out to the lake?" Thorbjorn guessed.

"I put him in the creek to stop him from screaming," Solvi said. "And when that was done, I let him go. I didn't care what happened to him after that. I did not try to hide his body."

"You didn't come to the council and explain what you did, either," Thorulv said, his voice a low growl.

"No, I did not," Solvi said, and he bowed his head to look down at his own hands. "I knew in that moment that I would have to leave. So why explain? I wanted only to finish one last piece. It was too big to carry with me, you see."

I sat back on my rock seat with a sigh, then looked up at Thorbjorn. "Are we missing any details, do you think?"

"I think he told us everything," Thorbjorn said. Unlike Solvi, his voice was thick with passion. He was angry.

I turned back to Solvi, who was still studying his own hands. "Your boon?" I asked.

"I ask only to be allowed to exile myself," he said. "I will continue down this path, deeper into the hills to where our people never go. And I will never return."

"You wish to escape punishment for what you have done?" Thorbjorn demanded.

Solvi shook his head.

"He wishes to choose his punishment," Thorulv said.

"That is for the volva to do," Thorbjorn said. I looked up at the other Thors, expecting one of them to argue that it was a matter for the council to decide, but they were all nodding their agreement. Even Thorulv.

"What I pronounce here and now shall be his fate?" I asked.

"We will see it done, volva," Thorulv said.

I folded my arms and thought it over. From what I knew, the council would be angry with Solvi for violating the trade rules, although they might go easy on him because of how careful he had been with that. But for the murder of a resident of Runde? I didn't think they would be inclined to punish that at all. Perhaps in other circumstances, but in this case, when Garrett Nelsen had so clearly violated an agreement and then invited retribution by laughing in the face of Solvi's grievances? No, I didn't think they would be too harsh with him. His request for self-exile was likely the harsher fate.

But now I was in the same place I had been before, knowing I had solved a Runde murder, but having no way to bring the culprit to justice. Now there'd be yet another family who would never know what had happened or why.

They'd never know that the murderer wasn't running free. How could they ever feel safe?

But there was nothing I could decide here on the rocky hillside that would solve that problem. Perhaps the Thors would put Solvi in chains if I asked and drag him to Runde where the police could pick him up, but what then? In exchange for one murderer facing justice, I would destroy the safety of everyone else in Villmark.

No, granting Solvi's boon was the best path before me. But it didn't sit well with me at all.

"You will leave this place and never be seen again," I said. "I have your word on that?"

"My word as a Villmarker, as a descendant of true Northmen, and as an artist," he said.

That last hit a special chord in me, as much as I wished it didn't. "Garrett Nelsen's plans to mass produce your work, I can be sure that those are stopped," I said. I was less sure than I was hopeful, but I had some thoughts on that score. I was pretty confident that Kyle would listen to them in due time.

"Thank you," Solvi said with a grateful bow.

"But in return I will need the rest of your work," I said. "Everything in your home and around it."

"It is yours," Solvi said. "My home, and everything in it, and everything around it, I now declare yours." Then he went on, "I regret that I killed Nelsen. But I regret more that Nelsen made it necessary. I believe selling my art has already enriched his people more than they deserve. I have nothing more to give them."

"Fair enough," I said. Then I waved my hand to dismiss him. "Be gone with you."

We six stood together on that hilltop until Solvi's form went from a silhouette to a blur to a mere dot. And then even that disappeared over one of an infinite number of hills.

"Do you think we'll ever see him again?" I asked. I was looking up at Thorbjorn, but it was Thorulv who answered.

"He'll be dead by this time tomorrow," he said and spat on the ground. "Thorbjorn, you can see the volva safely home?"

"Surely," Thorbjorn said.

"Thanks for answering our call," I said as the other brothers prepared to disperse.

"We'll always be here when you need us," Thorulv said. Thormund raised his spear in agreement, Thorge let out a battle-cry that was more terrifying than heartening, and Thoralv put out his fist and left it there until I bumped it with my own fist.

And then they were gone.

CHAPTER 25

$\mathcal{N}$ow that it was finally starting to get cold during the day, I could've wished for a few more warm Indian summer days. But as I stopped my work to sit for a moment on one of the benches and warm my hands over the flames of the fire-pit, I decided that it wasn't so bad. With Loke and Thorbjorn's help, it had only taken the better part of a day to load all of Solvi's moveable art onto the two wagons we had brought down from Villmark. And at least it hadn't started raining, which had looked like a real possibility when I had woken up that morning.

"I still don't get it," Loke said as he sat down across from me and peeled off his gloves to hold his palms toward the fire.

"What don't you get?" I asked.

"That bear," he said, pointing his chin towards the last sculpture which Thorbjorn was tying down on top of the load on one of the wagons. "You said he intended to leave after he killed Garrett Nelsen, but then he hung around to finish that. But no one was waiting for it. He just left it here in the yard."

"With the stain still wet," I said.

"But it wasn't promised to anybody," Loke persisted. "So why did he *have* to finish it?"

"To leave a task half done is a torture for some of us," I said. I didn't add, but secretly had thought since the moment Solvi had vanished from my sight, that he knew not only was he never coming back, but that he was about to walk to his inevitable death. Finishing the sculpture had given him just a little bit of time to come to terms with that decision.

Or so I believed. Now that he was gone and I couldn't ask him, I'd never really know.

"And I'm still mad you went past the tallest hill and fought with trolls and everything without asking me along," he sulked.

"I went to the top of the tallest hill, not past it," I corrected him. "And I could scarcely invite you when I don't know where you live."

"Did you ask for directions? Because anyone in Villmark could tell you where to go to find me," he said, still pouting. "Not to mention your cat. He can always find me. He stops by all the time."

"Hey, I asked you to go with me to the fire cave to try my magic, and you said no," I reminded him.

"That was different," he said.

"Well, the one led to the other with no time to look around and wonder if I should be issuing any invitations," I said. "And honestly, you want me to rely on my cat to get in contact with you? I don't know where *he* is half the time."

"If you need me, he'll know," Loke said. "He'll find you."

"Oh, stop," I said, pressing my hands to my temples. "I can't stand one more mystery. And don't you dare say I'll understand it all later, or someday, or when my memory magically decides to reappear. I just can't anymore."

"All right, Ingy," he said, and his voice was surprisingly gentle. I raised my head to look him in the eye. Was that sincerity there in their chocolate brown depths?

"All right what?" I asked, still suspicious.

"All right, I'll show you my house," he said. He got up and moved around the fire pit to sit next to me on the same bench, as if he didn't want Thorbjorn to overhear. "My parents died when I was ten and my sister was five. We've been on our own since then. I don't spend much time in that house. Too many memories. But if you like, when we are done with all this and have a bit of time, I'll show you which house."

"You have a sister?" I asked. It was hard to imagine. I wondered what she was like?

"Her name is Esja," he said. "As little as I like being home, she likes going out even less. But I shall be happy to introduce you two to each other. I'm not keeping secrets from you, Ingrid. There are just some things that hurt to speak of."

"I would love to meet your sister," I said. "But can I ask one more question?" A strand of hair had gotten loose from my knit cap and I brushed at it with the back of my hand, but it fell back into my eyes to twist up with my eyelashes. Loke reached out to gently untangle it, then tuck it behind my ear.

"Ask," he said.

"What's your name, really?"

I watched his face and eyes cascade through a series of emotions. Had the question surprised him? Was he entertaining the thought of not answering? Of telling me off for prying?

I definitely saw the moment when he flirted with getting out of answering by playing it all off as a joke.

But then he grew serious again. He gestured for me to lean closer, then whispered in my ear, "Loke Grímsson, at your service."

I leaned back to look him in the eye again. "That is a secret, isn't it?" He shrugged that careless shrug, but I knew he was only pretending not to care. "Why?"

"Names have power," he told me. "Some names have more power than others."

"But doesn't everybody know your name? You live in town, right? People knew your parents?" I asked.

He was about to answer but straightened suddenly, moving back on the bench to put more space between us the instant before Thorbjorn came around the corner of the house to join us.

"We're all set to ride into town," he said, but then stopped, looking at Loke and I suspiciously. "What's going on?"

"Nothing," I said. "Let's take one last pass through the house before we go to be sure we're not missing anything."

Thorbjorn nodded and held out a hand to help me off the bench. Perhaps he thought I didn't notice the hard glare he shot at Loke. It was certainly hard to miss Loke's mocking laugh.

I looked around the little cottage, but nothing had been missed. The fact was, most of the furniture was simply too big to fit through the door without being broken to pieces first, and that felt like a sacrilege. So we had left it untouched.

"It's a pity," I said.

"What's a pity?" Thorbjorn asked.

"That we can't take the rest with us. I mean, someone would really love this bed," I said, running my hands over the smooth wood.

"Someone does love it," he said, sounding confused. "You love it."

"I know, but I could never fit it in my grandmother's loft," I said. "Still, I've sketched everything, and taken photographs. That will have to be enough."

"Ingrid, Solvi gave you this house," Thorbjorn said. He still sounded confused. Heck, *I* was confused.

"No, I only asked for the art," I said. "I needed to give Kyle Meeks enough to get his shop running, so that he can pay off the debts Garrett Nelsen ran up in their business's name and pay the fees for canceling those manufacturing orders."

"That's all you asked for, but that's not all he gave you," Thorbjorn said.

I frowned but cast my mind back to that night on the hilltop. What had Solvi said, exactly?

"He did," I said, looking from Thorbjorn to Loke who was smirking as he leaned in the doorway. "He did, didn't he? This place is mine. All of this gorgeous woodwork is mine."

"It suits you," Loke said, looking around the interior. "And look, Mjolner has already made himself at home."

I gave Loke a puzzled look, but he was pointing at the bed. I peeked inside to see my cat curled up on the pillow, napping away. When had he arrived? And how?

"But it's not like I can live here," I said. "This place is in the woods. That's still off limits, right?"

"When I'm not with you, yes," Thorbjorn said. "But that won't always be true. Your power grows by the day."

"Well, by the month, maybe," Loke said, but we both ignored him.

"This is really mine," I said again, because it was so hard to believe it. I had never really imagined what my first place would be like, if I ever lived on my own. I had never wanted to leave my chronically ill mother on her own. If I had I might've imagined a garden level apartment somewhere. Or maybe a loft in the arty part of Minneapolis. But this? "This is amazing."

Loke was grinning at me like I was a dopey fool, which I supposed was how I was acting. But then he usually grinned like that at everyone, so what did it matter?

"Come," Thorbjorn said, clapping his hands together. "Fetch your cat. We have to get these wagons back to Villmark before it gets dark."

I picked up Mjolner and followed Thorbjorn to one of the wagons. Loke drove his on ahead, and when Thorbjorn got our horse to follow I turned back to keep the cottage in sight for as long as I could. Until the trees around us closed together to block it from view.

But it was still there and always would be. And it was mine.

CHAPTER 26

I don't have to be doing magic to lose all sense of time while doing art. Just getting caught up in the drawing can do it, especially if I'm working in ink and not pencil, which I was doing the afternoon before my grandmother and I were planning to have dinner with Lisa Sorensen's parents.

I had been nervous about how the evening was going to go, so to distract myself I had started working on a new illustration, something based on one of my sketches from the day out on the lake on the Viking ship. I liked the broad outline I had sketched out, but really got focused on the details of every single rower, of the carving on the prow and the pattern on the sail.

I was vaguely aware of the rich smell of my grandmother's butter cookies in the oven. But even the promise of that decadent goodness wasn't enough to pull me out of my mental world.

But her voice calling my name did. And she hadn't even put any magical oomph on it.

"Coming!" I called back, capping my ink and wiping my pen before running down the stairs. I was dressed to go, but my ink-stained fingers would probably need some explaining, or at least a sheepish apology. My fingers hadn't been clean, really clean, since I was a kid and moved beyond crayons.

But my grandmother wasn't waiting for me, cookie dish in hand, prepared to head out the door. She had called me for another reason all together, I realized as I rounded the landing on the stairs and saw three people sitting around the fireplace.

They looked up as they heard me approaching. I recognized Tore Nelsen straight away, but the other two were less familiar. Then I placed them: Garrett Nelsen's parents. I had seen their picture in the paper with the last story about his mysterious death.

"Oh. Hello," I said, slowing my steps down the last of the stairs. "I didn't realize we were expecting company?"

"Not expecting," my grandmother said, waving for me to take a seat beside her on the sofa. The three Nelsens sat together on the other sofa, the coffee table between us. Tore reached for the mug in front of him and took a sip of coffee, then wiped his lips nervously on his sleeve.

"I need to be here for this?" I whispered to my grandmother. Since I had done that bit of magic on the hilltop with my voice, I had discovered all sorts of things I could do. Like this particular ventriloquist trick, where my lips didn't move and only my grandmother could hear me.

"They're here for you, not me," she whispered back to me in the same way.

The three Nelsens were getting more uncomfortable by the second at the awkward silence. I cleared my throat, then offered them a polite smile. "What can I do for you?"

Inwardly, I chanted to myself, "please don't have a case. Please don't have a case. Please don't have a case."

Because I had gained a bit of a reputation around Runde for being a first-class investigator. Not for solving murders, of course. No one in Runde save my grandmother and Loke knew I had done that. Twice.

No, after bringing all of Solvi's art down from Villmark and giving it to Kyle, word had gotten out that all the poking around I had been doing after the murder had led me to a hidden stash of Garrett Nelsen's art. Now people wanted me to find all sorts of lost objects. Like I was the neighborhood bloodhound or something.

But somehow I doubted that was why Garrett Nelsen's parents wanted to see me. Surely that topic would be too painful for them?

"Miss Torfa," Tore said. "We wanted to thank you for what you did, finding those things that Garrett left behind."

"I just lucked upon it, really," I said, hoping they didn't press for details. Unlike Loke, I was terrible at remembering all the little things that would keep my lies consistent.

"Well, we were thinking maybe you could dig around some more," Tore said, casting a sideways glance at the other two who huddled closer together, their heads bowed over their entwined hands.

"You did?" I asked, skeptical. I couldn't imagine anyone who wanted to be where they were less than Garrett's parents.

"Yes. And of course there'd be a finder's fee," Tore said in a rush.

"I didn't collect a finder's fee the first time. Why would I want one now?" I asked.

"Of course," he said, mopping at his brow. "But you know we would've given you one, if you'd brought what you found to us and not to Kyle Meeks."

All of a sudden, I didn't like where this conversation was going. "I don't think so," I said, trying to keep my tone diplomatic. "Honestly, there is nothing more to be found. You should just make your peace with that."

"Well, maybe that's true and maybe that isn't," Tore said. I shot a look at my grandmother, who understood me at once. She got to her feet and headed towards the door.

"I am sorry, but Ingrid and I have another engagement we really shouldn't be late for," she said as she opened the door wide and waited for them to exit.

"Of course," Tore said again. "We didn't mean to intrude. We'll take this up another time, perhaps."

"No, we won't," I said. Tore, halfway between sitting and standing, froze and looked up at me, startled by the sudden change in my tone. I leaned forward over the coffee table to look him in the eye. "Mr. Nelsen, you got the money you needed for your bridge. Not that you ever needed that bridge. But what's done is done. Let it go."

He blinked at me but said nothing.

I looked over at Garrett's parents, who were still leaning on each other for support. I had a hunch they hadn't wanted to come here at all. But they had let Tore talk them into it.

"Mr. and Mrs. Nelsen," I said, and got the diplomatic back in my tone somehow. "I'm sorry for your loss. But the truth is, you know and I know that none of that work was ever really Garrett's. The true artist isn't going to make a fuss about credit. The little memorial for Garret and that anonymous artist's work will remain in the shop in Grand Marais. He'll be remembered, if only for a little while. But there is no more art. Do you understand?"

They nodded at me mutely.

"Good," I said. Then I looked to Tore. "We won't discuss this again."

"No, of course not," he said, and scurried out of the door with all haste.

My grandmother murmured condolences to the Nelsen parents, then closed the door behind them.

"I'm not sure if that's how I would've handled that," she said to me. But I couldn't tell from her tone or the expression on her face if she was disappointed or impressed.

"We're late," I said.

The October night made for a cold walk, but there was no wind coming in off the lake. Still, it was a surprise when Mrs. Sorensen sat us down around a table set out on their deck overlooking the moonlit lake. But they had heaters running all around us, and it was just warm enough not to be uncomfortable. And the stars scattered across the clear skies overhead made it well worth it.

The Sorensens seemed to be doing better. No longer numb with grief, they were pleasant company. Mrs. Sorensen had a wonderful laugh, and Mr. Sorensen delighted in saying and doing anything to provoke that laugh.

Still, people can put on a happy face in public. And most of Runde was deeply invested in always showing my grandmother their very best faces.

When we were done and the temperature was finally sinking low enough for us to feel it, Mrs. Sorensen started to get up to begin gathering up the dishes, but her husband got up first, putting a hand on her shoulder to keep her in her chair.

"You did all the cooking. I'll get the mess," he said, and she gave in with another little laugh.

"I'll help," my grandmother said, shooting me a look that told me I was going to be staying in my chair with Mrs. Sorensen. I wanted to complain about the cold and point out that twice the hands would make half the work, but I said nothing. There was no arguing with one of my grandmother's silent commands.

So I found myself alone with Mrs. Sorensen, looking out over the lake, the light from the moon reflecting off the currently gentle waves.

"How are you doing, really?" I asked her, my voice more earnest than I had meant for it to be. The last thing I wanted was for her to feel like I was interrogating her.

But she didn't take it that way at all. She just gave me a soft smile. "Well, we still miss Lisa. We'll always miss Lisa. But we're doing all right."

"It must be hard," I said, picking at a spot of gravy that had dried on the tablecloth so that I wouldn't have to look right at her. "I've heard the police aren't really investigating the case anymore."

"They've done their best," she said with a forced brightness. "They followed every lead they had. I believe them when they tell me that. And if they get any new leads, why, they'll pursue them as well. But without any leads, there isn't much that they can do."

I nodded. I was going to have to let this go. Asking more questions was going to hurt Mrs. Sorensen more than it was going to help me, I was sure. But it was hard, letting go.

"I know you never really met her, but I feel like if you had, you would've been friends," Mrs. Sorensen said, giving my hand a squeeze.

"I think so too," I said, but my voice choked on me.

She smiled a sad smile at me. "You take it hard. Like Jessica. Jessica takes it so hard. I try to talk to her, but I don't think she's ready to hear me yet."

"Jessica?" I asked.

She nodded. "I try to tell her, I know Lisa is at peace. I can feel it. Sometimes I dream about her too. But it doesn't feel like a normal dream. It's different. Maybe that sounds silly to you."

"No," I said.

"No? Well, you're an artist. Maybe that makes you more open to things."

I smiled at the irony. Being an artist was *not* what made me more open to these sorts of things. But I could scarcely say that out loud.

"If I had evidence, I could share it with Jessica, but I don't. I just have a feeling. And a hope that one day Jessica will come to feel the same. That Lisa loved us and misses us, but that at the core, she's found peace. And so should we, however we can."

Peace. It wasn't closure. But if her parents could find a way to make do with one without the other, could Jessica? Would it be enough for Jessica?

Would it be enough for me, if that was all I had to give people?

"Come," Mrs. Sorensen said, pushing herself up out of her chair and extending a hand to me. "Let's go inside. I can smell your grandmother's butter cookies from here, and there's no way I'm going to let my husband eat all those without us."

"I'm right behind you," I said. "I'll just switch off the heaters?"

"Turn the knob on the front all the way to the left," she said. "Thank you, dear."

I moved from heater to heater, switching them each off. I hadn't realized they had been making a low hum until they were all silent and I could hear the waves lapping against the shore. I stopped for a moment to watch those waves, leaning against the deck railing with my hands tucked inside my own sleeves.

I guess I knew now why my grandmother had set up this dinner. Not to check up on the Sorensens like she'd told me. No, she was checking up on me.

I could imagine what she would say, that Mrs. Sorensen wasn't deluding herself feeling like Lisa was at peace. Because my grand-mother and I knew for a fact that her spirit was at peace. We had sensed that in the very first magic lessons we had done together. After the murder had been solved and Halldis had been locked away, Lisa had stopped haunting me. If you could call what she had been doing to me "haunting."

And somehow, without having a hint of magic in her body, Mrs. Sorensen knew it too. I hadn't gotten credit for solving the murder, and I hadn't given her closure, but my actions had given her peace.

Well, it wasn't nothing.

A shiver ran over me as I stood there just looking up at the moon, and I hurried back inside the house, where warmth and coffee and rich butter cookies awaited me.

CHECK OUT BOOK THREE!

The Viking Witch will return in Murder on the Lake, available now!

Ingrid Torfa juggles two very different lives. In one she lives as an aspiring book illustrator in a quiet old fishing village on the North Shore of Lake Superior.

But in the other she lives as an apprentice volva, a Viking Witch, in a lost Norse village that exists half in and half out of the real world.

Balancing those two lives is trouble enough. But then a murder forces her to work in both worlds at once. She needs all her friends to help her solve this case.

But first, they all have to meet. And half of them are about to get their minds blown.

Murder on the Lake, book 3 in the Viking Witch Cozy Mystery series.

Murder on the Lake, Book 3 in the Viking Witch Mystery Series!

THE WITCHES THREE COZY
MYSTERIES

In case you missed it, check out Charm School, the first book in the complete Witches Three Cozy Mystery Series!

Amanda Clarke thinks of herself as perfectly ordinary in every way. Just a small-town girl who serves breakfast all day in a little diner nestled next to the highway, nothing but dairy farms for miles around. She fits in there.

But then an old woman she never met dies, and Amanda was named in her will. Now Amanda packs a bag and heads to the big city, to Miss Zenobia Weekes' Charm School for Exceptional Young Ladies. And it's not in just any neighborhood. No, she finds herself on Summit Avenue in St. Paul, a street lined with gorgeous old houses, the former homes of lumber barons, railroad millionaires, even the writer F. Scott Fitzgerald. Why, Amanda can practically hear the jazz music still playing across the decades.

Scratch that. The music really, literally, still plays in the backyard of the charm school. Because the house stretches across time itself. Without a witch to protect this tear in the fabric of the world, anything can spill over. Like music.

Or like murder.

Charm School, the first book in the complete Witches Three Cozy Mystery Series!

ALSO FROM RATATOSKR PRESS

The Ritchie and Fitz Sci-Fi Murder Mysteries starts with Murder on the Intergalactic Railway.

For Murdina Ritchie, acceptance at the Oymyakon Foreign Service Academy means one last chance at her dream of becoming a diplomat for the Union of Free Worlds. For Shackleton Fitz IV, it represents his last chance not to fail out of military service entirely.

Strange that fate should throw them together now, among the last group of students admitted after the start of the semester. They had once shared the strongest of friendships. But that all ended a long time ago.

But when an insufferable but politically important woman turns up murdered, the two agree to put their differences aside and work together to solve the case.

Because the murderer might strike again. But more importantly, solving a murder would just have to impress the dour colonel who clearly thinks neither of them belong at his academy.

Murder on the Intergalactic Railway, the first book in the Ritchie and Fitz Sci-Fi Murder Mysteries.

FREE EBOOK!

Like exclusive, free content?

If you'd like to receive "The Cat's Hammer," a free prequel short story to the Viking Witch Cozy Mystery series, plus a ton of other free goodies, go to CateMartin.com to subscribe to my monthly newsletter! This eBook is exclusively for newsletter subscribers and will never be sold in stores. Check it out!

ABOUT THE AUTHOR

Cate Martin is a mystery writer who lives in Minneapolis, Minnesota.

ALSO BY CATE MARTIN

The Witches Three Cozy Mystery Series

Charm School

Work Like a Charm

Third Time is a Charm

Old World Charm

Charm his Pants Off

Charm Offensive

The Viking Witch Cozy Mystery Series

Body at the Crossroads

Death Under the Bridge

Murder on the Lake

Killing in the Village Commons (coming February 9, 2021)